Praise for *The World is (Not) a Cold Dead Place*

'Dark, funny, shitty, violent, moving.'
James Brown, *talkSPORT*

'A beautiful bruise of a book. Nathan O'Hagan is a voice to
reckon with.'
Russ Litten, author of *Kingdom*

'Nathan O'Hagan is a very talented writer.'
Kevin Sampson, author of *Awaydays*

ALSO BY NATHAN O'HAGAN

Purge
The World is (Not) a Cold Dead Place

Connect with Nathan:

Twitter: @NathanOHagan
www.nathanohagan.weebly.com
www.facebook.com/NathanOHaganwriter/

Out of the City

Nathan O'Hagan

Published by Armley Press 2017
ISBN 978-0-9934811-6-1

Acknowledgements
Copy-editing: John Lake
Layout: Ian Dobson
Production: Mick McCann
Cover design: Mick Lake & Rob Appleby
Cover photo: Tim Hyde
Epigrams: lyrics by Ian Curtis

Thanks to Mick McCann, John Lake, Mick Lake, Wayne Leeming, Mark Connors (the Armley Press gang), James Brown, James Endeacott, Rob Appleby, The Smudgester and, most importantly, my loving and supportive family

"Existence, well what does it matter? I exist on the best terms I can."

PART ONE: DAMAGED GOODS

ONE

Nick checked his watch. 2:17am. He slid his chair back and stretched his legs out as much as the interior of his car allowed. Two hours. Two hours he had been waiting. He lit up another cigarette. He was cramped, tired and cold, his bladder aching and full. He picked up one of the empty paper coffee cups at his feet. He undid his fly, took his dick out and pissed into it. He wound down his window and tipped the piss out. He checked his watch. 2:43am. He took out his hipflask, a quick drop to steady his nerves for the task in hand. He felt his eyes closing. He slapped himself hard across the face and tried to shake the sleepiness out. He stretched his eyelids out with his fingers. He pinched the skin on his neck hard between his thumb and forefinger. The pain jolted him awake for about half a minute, before the sleepiness came back. Nick checked his watch again. 3:16am. Fuck this shit. Ten more minutes. Ten more minutes and he was gone. Nick lit another cigarette and waited. He turned the key in the ignition just as a black cab passed him and pulled up at Gambier Terrace. He switched the engine off and watched as a lanky figure stumbled out of the taxi and went into the building. Nick waited till the cab was out of sight and got out of his car. He flicked his cigarette down a grid, checked the street in both directions, took a deep breath and walked over to the large Georgian town house, now divided into flats. He used his elbow to press the doorbell for the ground floor flat. No going back now. A few seconds passed and the heavy front door was opened.

"Nick Hanman, as I live and breathe. Get your fucking arse into that flat of mine, me old son," Francis Berry said, stepping back to allow Nick to enter. "A rare pleasure these days."

Nick put a finger to his lips to shush him, and nodded

9

towards his flat. Nick clocked the tinny techno coming from the flat above. He walked into Francis's flat, and Francis closed the door behind them.

"Looking suave as ever, Mr Hanman," Francis said, admiring Nick's suit. "Ted Baker?"

"Of course."

"Nice. Very nice. So what's your desire tonight then, Nick? Pills or powder?"

"Neither tonight."

"You on the wagon again?"

"Two months now," Nick said, nodding.

"A record for you, I do believe."

Francis sat down and leaned over his coffee table, fiddling with a half-rolled joint.

"I trust you won't mind if I partake whilst we parlay?"

"Go ahead," Nick replied, sitting down opposite him.

"So what can I do for thee?"

"Michael Epson."

Francis's hands stopped dead at the mention of the name, then started to shake fractionally as he continued to skin up.

"Who?" he asked.

"Oh, you don't know who he is?"

Francis pretended to search his memory.

"Can't say's I do, Nick. Can't say's I do."

"Oh, well, then, allow me to enlighten you," Nick said, standing up. He walked slowly around the room as he continued. "Michael Epson is something of a legend round these parts, so I'm *really* surprised you haven't heard of him. From a working class family in Bootle, he started off selling fruit and veg at The Strand. From there he built his way up, opened more shops, eventually opening them up at rate of one a month county-wide, then went national."

Nick stopped and leaned towards Francis.

"Please do stop me if this is jogging your memory, won't you?"

Francis shook his head weakly. Nick continued his speech, and his wandering around the room.

"He diversified, grew his businesses and made his first million by the time he was twenty-eight. Bear in mind, if you will, Francis, this was back in the days when to make a million really meant something. Long before any jammy cunt with a half decent house could practically become a millionaire overnight. A real rags to riches story. Heartwarming stuff, it really is. And of course, with money comes influence and power. Before long Michael had become one of the wealthiest, most important men in Liverpool. But he's not afraid to put his hand in his pocket. He's known for his generosity, in fact, making large, regular contributions to local charities. Quite the philanthropist. Unsurprisingly, the people of Liverpool came to love him. He was even awarded the freedom of the city, an honour bestowed upon only a lucky few. The *Echo* even called him the unofficial mayor of the city."

"Fascinating stuff, mate. Somebody should make a film about him or something. But what's this got to do with me?"

"Oh, well, I'm glad you asked, Francis, I'm glad you asked. See, despite all this wealth, the power, the influence, the adulation, the big home and the beautiful family, old Michael has, like the rest of us, a weakness. And his weakness is that he just can't help paying young rent boys to let him suck on their youthful cocks."

"Oh well, to each his own, I say."

"Oh, indeed, Francis, indeed. But unfortunately, having this particular predilection leaves a man like Michael very vulnerable. Say, to some scuzzy, small-time, drug-dealing lowlife acquiring photographs of Michael with his lips wrapped round some nice, hard, teen cock, and then using said photographs to blackmail some money out of him."

Francis put the incomplete spliff down and sank back into the couch. Nick stopped walking and stood behind him.

"And then, to compound it, after Mr Epson has paid the money in a timely fashion as instructed, no questions asked, quite contrary to the advice of his personal security consultant, this drug-dealing deviant then demands *even more* money. Can you believe that?"

Francis said nothing.

"That was unbelievably fucking stupid, Francis."

"So what happens now, then?"

"Well, whatever does happen, Francis, just remember that you brought it on yourself."

As Nick spoke he pulled a plastic bag from his pocket and wrapped it tightly round Francis's face. His standing position gave him the leverage he needed. His grip tightened as Francis struggled. He heard his own name, muffled through the bag, as Francis begged him to stop. He saw the plastic cling to Francis's mouth and nostrils as he desperately fought for breath, the plastic tightening as he sucked in what little air was in the bag. Francis made feeble attempts to reach behind himself and grab at Nick, getting only handfuls of jacket. Nick felt his arms starting to weaken just as Francis began to thrash his legs violently, the bag looking like a grotesque plastic mask against his face. Nick redoubled his efforts and was relieved to feel Francis finally begin to slacken. He took one last big breath in and lifted his feet up off the floor, allowing his own bodyweight to provide the last of the tenacity he needed. A few more seconds, and Francis, at last, went limp. Nick let go and let the body slump onto its side on the couch. He sat down on the floor to catch his breath. When he was ready he put on his gloves and dragged the body over to the bed and stripped it naked. He took another plastic bag from his pocket and emptied its contents around the body: some lube, a bottle of poppers, condoms. As a final touch, he tied the wrists behind the back with some gaffer tape, which he also used to secure the bag around Francis's neck. Nick gave the room a quick scan. It was sufficient. Not perfect, but Nick figured nobody would waste too much effort examining the scene. Not for a scumbag like Francis. He opened the door of the flat and listened for any movement from the other flats. All he could hear was the same tinny techno. He stepped back inside and eased the door shut again. He lifted the cushions off the couch and pulled back the fabric underneath them. There, in neat little bundles, were several large piles of cash, wrapped tightly

12

in plastic. Nick took them out and stuffed them into his pockets. He walked back to the front door but before he left he walked back into the flat and over to the table and helped himself to a jar of pills and a bag of coke.

TWO

".....ninety-eight, ninety-nine, one hundred."

Scott Collins let the dumbbells drop noisily to the floor, letting out a roar as he did so. He felt the burn of lactic acid flow through his muscles. Bicep curls. Thirty kilograms in each hand. A hundred reps. Ten sets. Followed by the same amount of tricep curls. He walked over to the leg press machine. He was always careful not to neglect his legs. He tended to concentrate most of his efforts on his upper body, particularly his pecs. This was a trap that amateur bodybuilders often fell into. Generally, only a pro builder had the discipline to steer clear of these pitfalls, but Scott possessed the kind of focus needed. That being said, his arms had certainly been his main focus in the last week or so, and they were looking more sculpted than ever. His shoulders were beautifully rounded, his triceps and biceps defined. A total of over five hundred shoulder lifts with thirty kilograms every day for the last fortnight had seen to that. He now wore a vest to the gym, where he had once worn T-shirts. He had worked hard to get his shoulders and upper arms looking this good, he might as well show them the fuck off. Now he moved the pin down to seventy-five kilograms and pushed with both feet. A couple of hundred reps here, then he would hit the treadmill. He had a tendency to get too beefcake at times, putting everything into his upper body, his traps. He was leaning that way now, but he felt OK about it. He liked the way he was looking, but a solid half-hour run to burn a few hundred calories seemed like a good way to finish off a superb morning's work. He wanted his upper body big and toned, but his midsection lithe. That was always a hard balance to strike, but he was averaging at least a thousand stomach crunches a day. Two hundred and fifty when he woke up and another two fifty before bed, with a few other sets spread throughout the day. His abs hadn't looked this good in years. His glutes were firm, his calf and thigh muscles were getting there. They weren't perfect, but they had improved a lot over the last month. The hard work was paying off.

In the locker room he stepped out of the shower and stood in front of the full-length mirror. He flexed and tightened each muscle group in turn. He quickly checked between the rows of lockers to make sure he was alone. He took off his towel and stood naked before the mirror. He looked at his reflection. He looked at his cock. Five inches on the slack, over nine when he was hard. He took it in his hand and jerked it a few times. Not so it was hard, just so it hung that bit lower. A nice bit of heft to it. He looked good. He looked *really fucking good*. He turned to the side, first to his left, then to his right. He turned his back to the mirror and looked back over his shoulder. He tensed his arse and flexed his arms. There was a beautiful symmetry from this angle that he couldn't stop staring at. He unflexed and flexed again. His lats needed a bit more work. They looked good, better than most of the fucking lightweights in his gym, but not as good as the rest of him. A set of five hundred reps on the lat pulldown as soon as he got here tomorrow. Then another set of the same after he'd repeated today's workout. He heard the door to the locker room open, and quickly picked his towel up. Just as he wrapped it round his waist, one of the gym faggots walked in. One of the group of them that usually worked out at weekends and spent too much time on their pecs and not enough on their shoulders. He looked at Scott. Scott stared him down until he looked away. Fucking dirty shit-stabber. Scott walked to his locker and checked the faggot wasn't watching him. When he was sure he wasn't being watched he took out some Dianabol. Twenty milligrams. He knocked it back with the protein shake he'd brought with him. He dressed and left.

THREE

Nick eased through the front door and slipped his shoes off. The third stair creaked as he stepped on it. No matter how many times he attempted a stealthy entrance, he always forgot about the third fucking stair. He crept up to the bathroom, closed the door and switched on the light. Nick undressed and folded his clothes on top of the laundry basket. He stood naked in front of the mirror. *Ecce homo.* He looked himself up and down until his gaze settled, as always, on the scar. A single, jagged line from underneath his right nostril, cutting diagonally across his philtrum and ending on the left side of his upper lip. Like a river cutting through a page of an atlas.

Christmas Eve, 1982. Nick heard his dad coming noisily in through the front door, singing.

"We wish you a merry Christmas, we wish you a merry Christmas," he sang, interrupted only by what sounded like him falling over the shoes by the front door.

"Shhhh," he heard his mum whisper, "you'll wake Nicky up." Then a sound he knew well, the sound of his dad's open palm against his mum's face.

"Don't fucking tell me to shush, woman."

"I'm sorry, I just didn't want Nicky waking up."

"That's a good idea, let's wake little Nicky up."

Nick heard his dad falling up the stairs and quickly turned to face the wall, shutting his eyes tightly. His bedroom door burst open, filling his room with a long shard of light from the landing. He shut his eyes even tighter.

"Come on, little man, wake up. It's Christmas Eve, come and have a drink with your dad." Nick pretended to be asleep, but it was no use. His dad shook him roughly and began to drag him out of bed.

"Come on, son, up you get." Nick was dragged downstairs, to where his mum was standing in the hallway.

"Please, John," she said, *"he's only seven, he should be in bed."* John took a big swig from the bottle of whiskey he was holding.

"Bollocks, it's Christmas Eve, he wants to come and have a drink with his dad. Here, have a swig of this, son," John shoved the bottle under Nick's nose. He knew that smell. And he hated it. He hated it on his dad's breath. He hated it when it had been spilled on the carpet after his dad had passed out while drinking it. And he hated it even more now the bottle was right under his nose. He turned his head away. His mum grabbed his other hand and tried to pull him away from his dad. A brief and clumsy tug of war ensued.

"Let him go, John. Look, he doesn't want a drink, he needs to be in bed." John let go of Nick's hand, sending Nick and his mum to the ground. John walked over to her and kicked her in the stomach. She curled herself into a ball to protect herself as he did it again.

"You remember who you're fucking talking to, woman. Don't you ever fucking undermine me in front of the boy again. Do you hear me, you fucking cunt?" She nodded her head silently. John grabbed Nick's hand and roughly dragged him to his feet. *"And you, have a fucking drink with your dad when you're told to."* He shoved the bottle right into his face, splitting his lip instantly. Nick tasted blood and whiskey. The antiseptic taste. The sharp sting as the whiskey seeped into the cut. He choked on blood and whiskey as his dad let him drop back to the floor.

"Some fucking family this is. Fuck the pair of you. Merry fucking Christmas." He put his coat back on and headed out the door.

Nick switched the bathroom light off and crept through to his bedroom. Lisa was turned on her side facing away from him. He slid into bed next to her as gently as he could.

"If you're trying not to wake me, don't bother," she said. "Where have you been?"

"Just working."

"Who for?"

"Does it matter?"

"It does when it means you ducking out of your own daughter's fourth birthday party early."

"Well exactly where do you think I get the money to pay for the parties? Where do you think I get the money to buy this house?"

Work wasn't the only reason he had left Monica's party early. They'd had a bunch of her friends round for a party. He'd hired a clown, bought wine and left some beers in a bucket of ice for the mums and dads. Nick had promised not to drink. He was two months sober, and didn't even feel like he wanted to. But as he manned the barbecue, he felt the thirst. He resisted for a while, but it was hot. Real beer-drinking weather. If he just had the one while he was flipping the burgers, just a single bottle... Just a Peroni. It's not even very strong, and it's just so light and refreshing. He couldn't see why he shouldn't just have the one. But one quickly became seven. Then he remembered the bottle of single malt he was going to take to his dad. He opened that and insisted that all the dads have a glass. He ignored Lisa's disapproving looks and refilled all their glasses, even those that didn't want any, filling his own glass with twice as much as everyone else had. By the time Monica blew out her candles, he was drunk enough for even her to notice. He walked clumsily to the downstairs toilet room, where he pissed messily over the seat and floor. As he washed his hands, he stared at his reflection. He realised then how drunk he was, and decided the best thing would be for him to go for a drive to clear his head. He felt his phone vibrating in his pocket and looked at the caller display: Michael Epson.

"Hello."

"Nick, are you busy?"

Nick heard the sound of children's laughter through the window.

"No. What do you need?"

"There's a mess I need you to clear up for me. A big

mess. Can I count on you, Nick?"

"Always."

That was over twelve hours ago. Since then he'd had time to sober up, and make his visit to the unfortunate Francis Berry.

"I was working, Lisa. That's all you need to know."

"Don't treat me like a fucking idiot, Nick."

"Well don't fucking act like one then."

"I beg your pardon?"

"Forget it."

Nick stood and grabbed his pillow.

"I'll sleep on the couch."

"Now who's acting like a fucking idiot?"

Nick was already out of the room before Lisa could finish the sentence. He went down to the living room and sat on the couch. He looked at his hands. They were trembling. He clenched his fists tight to try and stop them. They only trembled more. He stood up and went to the kitchen, where he was relieved to see that Lisa hadn't poured the rest of the whiskey away as he'd thought she would. He took a long, slow swig straight from the bottle. He began pouring the rest of it down the sink but stopped before the end and downed the last of it. He left it by the sink, hoping it would trick Lisa into thinking he had poured it all away.

Nick left the kitchen and walked to the bottom of the stairs. He looked up them, willing himself to go back up, he even put his foot on the bottom stair and left it there for a full half minute before finally retracting it. He walked back to the living room and sat down on the couch and began to sob. He grabbed a cushion and buried his face in it. He screamed into it. Again and again he screamed, wrapping the cushion around his head to swallow up the sound. He stood up and almost *ran* through the kitchen, into the utility room and through the door that connected it to the garage, got into the car and opened the glove box. He took out the bag of powder he'd taken from Francis's table and opened it. He dabbed his finger into it and touched it to his tongue. Smack. Not coke, as he'd thought – but smack probably suited his current needs better. He piled some onto the tip of his fingernail and lifted it to his nostril. He snorted it, left nostril then right. He did it again. And a third time. The fourth time, he only managed to get his finger halfway to his nostril before he felt it kick in. It was a feeling like no other, a heroin high. He loved coke, he loved pills and uppers, but at times like this, heroin brought him something that the other drugs didn't: sweet, dark oblivion.

FOUR

"Ha-ha-ha, you fucking fanny!"

Christian peeled his face off the tarmac and looked back up the thirty-six concrete steps. He had just slid down the metal banister on his skateboard, and was just feet from reaching the bottom when his board slipped, sending him clattering down the last few steps, landing face first at the bottom. He rolled onto his back, hitched himself up on his elbows and extended his index fingers to his mates at the top of the steps.

"Closer than any of you fuckers have got," he shouted to them, then rolled out of the way before being crushed by the next person to hit the ground attempting to ride that banister. He picked his board up and ran up the steps. He took the ciggie Tommo had been holding for him.

"Jeans are fucked, mate," Tommo said, nodding at Chris's knees. Chris looked down to see his knee, bloody and scraped, sticking out of his Bench jeans. He shrugged. "State of your elbow too, man." Chris angled his arm and neck so he could see the scuffed patch of raw skin, a trail of blood running down towards his wrist. "You'd best give that a wash."

"Yeah, I suppose so. Watch me board for me."

Chris walked over to the public toilet, where he stuck his bloody elbow under the running cold tap. He squeezed the last few pumps of soap from the dispenser and washed it as best he could, the sting of the soap in the wound hurting more than the impact of the fall initially had, though that pain was spreading quickly through his body now. Another can of Kestrel Super would hopefully kill that. He looked in the mirror. There was a scrape along his jawline, which he washed with the last of the soapy water. He checked his complexion, wet his fingers and ran them through his hair; bleached blond with dark roots coming through. He looked good. Those soft, almost feminine features and those bright, blue eyes that the girls all loved so much. He went into the toilet cubicle for a piss. He looked at the waist-high holes in each side of the cubicle walls. He saw the phone numbers, the graffiti: *be here 3 o'clock Thursdays to get your cock sucked*; *call 07924563027 if you want to fist my tight arse.* He felt dirty just being in there. He almost ran back to where his friends were. Tommo was trudging back up the steps looking like he'd just eaten even more shit than Chris had; his jeans were ripped and he was holding one battered arm in the other.

"Didn't even get halfway down before I came off the bar," he shouted to Chris.

"No way can anyone get to the bottom of that," someone else said.

Chris kicked his board up and caught it.

"Yeah? We'll fucking see about that."

*

Christian turned the corner into Leighton Grove. He leaned back on his board and let the gentle hill carry him down towards the McGann residence. He jumped off as he reached the gate, kicked up his board and carried it through the front door. His mum and dad, Emily and Billy, were sitting in the living room. Chris could hear the TV spewing out some soap opera or other. He popped his head around the door.

"Hiya," he said.

Emily looked around.

"Hello. You're a bit late, aren't you? I was expecting you back for dinner."

He shrugged his shoulders.

"Went skating instead."

Chris noticed his dad half turn his head towards him as though he was about to speak, but he just turned back to the TV.

"Well your dinner's in the oven."

"I'm not hungry."

"You should eat something, Chris."

"Maybe later. I'm gonna get a drink and go and listen to some music."

His dad spoke up this time.

"Not too loud," he said without moving his head.

Chris went to the kitchen and flicked the kettle on. He leant against the sideboard and played with his phone. He heard the living room door open and close. He kept looking at his phone, and the fact that not a word was said confirmed his suspicion that it was his dad. His mum would have said something, anything, to break the silence, whereas he and his dad were content to be in the same room without uttering a single word to each other. His dad opened the fridge and took another can of lager out. Chris heard the can fizz open.

"Look at the state of your jeans."

Chris looked down at the tear on his knee. He shrugged again.

"Doesn't matter," he said.

"It'll matter to me when you come to me wanting a new pair."

"I won't, they're fine."

"Fine? There's a big rip in them. Mind you, I suppose that just makes them cooler to you, doesn't it?"

Chris kept tapping away on his phone.

"Looks like your knee's even more scuffed than your jeans."

"It's just a scrape. I've had worse."

"Well get it washed, at least."

"It's fine."

"Alright then, don't. Leave it to bleed."

He walked back to the living room door, but stopped as he reached it.

"You can have a can if you like."

"Nah, I'm making a cup of tea."

"Alright, then."

He opened the living room door to go back in. Chris felt a twinge of guilt, and thanked his dad, but did so just as the living room door was closed again, leaving him unsure whether Billy would have heard him or not. He finished making his cup of tea and carried it up to his bedroom. He lay on his bed and pressed "play" on the stereo remote control. Biffy Clyro blasted out from it. He thought about what his dad had said and turned it down a touch.

*

Scott clicked on the link to the gangbang scene but found himself bored within a few seconds. Not rough enough. Too tame. He typed "rough anal" into the search bar and scrolled through the results. He'd seen half of these before, he recognised the girls' faces from the still photograph of each scene by the link. He kept scrolling and saw a scene he hadn't watched before. His mouse cursor hovered above the link for a while. Eventually he clicked on it and clicked the cursor onto the time bar, taking him two minutes into the clip. It was two men, one fucking the other. Hard. He clicked to take the clip five minutes further on. Now the guy was getting his cock sucked. Scott watched for a few seconds then closed the webpage down and slammed his laptop shut.

He walked through to the kitchen and switched the kettle on. As the kettle boiled he thought about the few seconds of the clip he had just watched. He tried to think about the other clips he'd watched, the ones with women, but couldn't remember much detail. The kettle whistled and clicked off as it reached boiling point. Scott stood there for a moment, watching the steam dissipate. He walked back to the front room, opened his laptop back up and searched again for the clip.

FIVE

"Daddy!"

Monica jumped down from the dinner table as soon as she heard the front door close. Nick threw his coat down and knelt to allow her to run into his arms. He gathered her up, lifting her effortlessly.

"Baby," he said, "how's my little munchkin?"

"She was doing very well with her dinner. Until now."

"Uh-oh, Daddy's in trouble," Nick said to Monica.

"Naughty Daddy!"

"Go on, better listen to Mummy and get back to the table."

Lisa glared at him. Just days ago they had a row about this. Nick being absent for long stretches, then waltzing in and getting to be the returning hero while she gets stuck with all the disciplining and running of the house. Now, he lifted his hands up in a placatory gesture and mouthed *sorry*. She shook her head and turned away. They were at that point now. The point where your every gesture was taken as an act of hostility by the other person. And, in all honesty, that was probably the case. For both of them. Even on those rare occasions when one or other of them made a conciliatory or humorous gesture or remark, it was nearly always misinterpreted by the other, the misinterpretation itself in turn becoming an act of aggression.

Nick lowered Monica to the floor and she ran back to the table. She practically skipped there. She was always so happy, it almost broke Nick's heart to look at her sometimes. She was so full of the purest kind of love and joy, and all he was full of was shit and poison. He was toxic by comparison, and he wondered how much he was corroding her just by being in the same room.

"Your dinner's in the microwave, just give it a minute."

"I'm not hungry."

"You need to eat."

"I'm alright."

"OK, fine. Don't eat."

Nick walked to the espresso machine and got himself a coffee. He sat down at the table opposite Monica.

"Where've you been, Daddy?"

"Yes, Daddy, where have you been?" Lisa repeated without looking in Nick's direction. Nick shot her a look but she didn't see it, she just kept watching Monica feed herself.

"Daddy's been out working, making money so I can buy nice things for you and Mummy."

"Ooh, I like nice things, Daddy."

"I know you do, baby, and so does Mummy."

"Yes, Monica," Lisa said, "of course, Daddy doesn't like nice things at all, he doesn't like fancy suits and cars, he doesn't do any of it for himself."

Lisa shook her head slightly. Nick wasn't sure if she was shaking her head at his comments or the realisation of what a pathetic cliché they had become. The cliché of the couple that argue through their children. Nick shook his own head.

"Let's not do this," he said, knowing that it was him that had started it.

"No, let's not."

This was said with a conciliatory tone. Nick decided to follow suit, partly because it was so rare for one of them to offer an olive branch to the other that it would be churlish of him not to. But he knew deep down that Lisa's gesture was also in part to ensure she kept the moral high ground.

"Are you going back out?"

"Probably not."

"You can do bath and bedtime then."

"OK."

"Yay, bedtime with Daddy," Monica said, clapping her hands.

Nick smiled at her. Out of the corner of his eye, he saw Lisa turn her head towards him. He looked at her and their eyes met. The beginnings of a small smile began to form in the corner of her mouth. However much simmering resentment there was between them, Monica was the one thing that still had the potential to unite them.

Brrrrr. Brrrrr. Brrrrr.

Nick's phone vibrated loudly on the table. Nick picked it up. He looked at the caller display: Gareth O'Connor's name was on the screen.

"Ignore it," Lisa said.

"I can't, it's work."

"Of course, what else would it be?"

"I need to get this."

"Fine."

"I'll get rid of them, it's probably nothing."

He walked into the living room and answered his phone.

"Nick? It's Gareth. I need your help, mate."

This clearly wasn't nothing. Gareth was one of Nick's newest clients, yet another account Epson had got for him. Gareth O'Connor, twenty-one years old, Premiership footballer, one of a couple of dozen or so footballers Nick was employed by as their "security consultant". Yet another stupid young lad thrust into unbelievable wealth by their footballing ability.

"What's wrong, Gareth?"

"Oh, fuck, man, this is bad. This is so fucking bad. I didn't know who else to call."

"Gareth, just calm down and tell me what's happened."

"I don't think she's breathing, Nick. She's not fucking breathing."

"Gareth. Listen to me, turn her onto her side, I'm coming over."

"Should I call an ambulance, Nick?"

"No, Gareth, just put her on her side. I'll be there in twenty minutes. Don't call anyone else. Do you hear me,

Gareth?"

"I hear you. Just fucking hurry, Nick, please."

Nick hung up and walked back into the kitchen. The look on Lisa's face told him she already knew what he was going to say. He picked up his jacket.

"I'm sorry, baby," he said to Monica. "Daddy's got to go out. Mummy will have to do bedtime tonight."

"Aw, no fair," she said, instantly crying.

"I'm so sorry, baby, I promise I'll do it tomorrow."

"Do *not* make promises like that when we both know you can't keep them," Lisa said, comforting her daughter.

"Look, it can't be helped, I *have* to go out. If it wasn't so important I wouldn't—"

"You wouldn't what, Nick? You wouldn't run out on your own daughter? You wouldn't leave her crying like this? Just go, Nick."

Nick did as he was instructed. He ran to the Range Rover Evoque and gunned it down the driveway and through the gates. Gareth O'Connor lived half an hour away, but Nick knew if luck was with him he could probably make it in less than twenty minutes. He swerved and slalomed through the idling midday traffic on the road out to Cheshire. There was always the chance he would get pulled over but, from the sounds of it, this situation was dire enough that it was worth the risk. He still didn't know what Gareth had done, but he had to weigh the chances of getting pulled over against the possibility of one of his clients soon having a dead body on his hands, which meant a dead body on Nick's hands. Easy decision. Nineteen minutes after leaving his own home he skidded into Gareth's driveway, stopping feet from the front door. Gareth instantly came running out, his face etched with fear.

"Oh, thank fuck, Nick, thank fuck."

"Where is she?"

"In the bedroom."

Nick took the stairs three at a time and ran into the huge bedroom. There on the bed, slumped on her side, was a young girl. She looked about seventeen. Eighteen, max.

"What the fuck have you given her, Gareth?"

"I haven't given her nothing, honest, Nick."

"What happened?"

"I don't know. Everything was fine last night. Then when I woke up she just wasn't moving, and I couldn't wake her up."

Nick performed a rudimentary check.

"Is she breathing, Nick?"

"Yeah. She's got a decent pulse too."

"So what the fuck's up with her?"

"I don't fucking know. Do you know if she's taken anything?"

"I don't think so. Not when I was with her."

Nick was turning her onto her back when something caught his eye, a small pendant around her neck. He leaned in close to read the inscription.

"What is it?" Gareth asked, his fingers laced together behind his head in anxiety.

"It's a medical-alert necklace."

"A what?"

"A medical-alert necklace."

"What the fuck's that?"

"It's something people with some medical conditions wear so people know what's wrong with them."

"So what's wrong with her?"

"She's diabetic."

"Oh fuck. Is that bad?"

"It's nowhere near as bad as it could have been."

"So what do we do?"

"I'm thinking."

"You're thinking? Fucking hell, Nick, what the fuck do I pay you for? What are we gonna do?"

"Shut the fuck up a minute, will you?"

"Oh, fuck this, I'm calling an ambulance."

Gareth walked across to the phone at the side of his bed.

"Hang on a minute."

"Fuck that, I need to get her the fuck out of here. I'm

29

calling an ambulance, and you're sacked. You've been fucking useless."

"Don't pick up that phone, Gareth."

Gareth picked the phone up and began to dial. Before he had finished dialling, Nick walked purposefully over to him and shoved his open hand into Gareth's throat. He instantly dropped the hand piece, which Nick caught in mid-air and replaced on the receiver. Gareth dropped to his knees, grabbing his throat.

"Now listen to me. Here's what's gonna happen. First, you're gonna calm the fuck down. Secondly, you're gonna help me carry her down to my car. Then, I'm gonna drive her to somewhere a few miles from here, somewhere with no CCTV, where I'm gonna leave her, before calling an ambulance for her."

"And what happens when she wakes up?" Gareth managed to choke the words out. "She'll go to the press, won't she? The papers'll make me look like a right scumbag."

"When she wakes up, I'll pay her a visit, and ensure she won't go to the papers."

"How the fuck are you gonna do that?"

"I'm gonna tell her that you will pay her treble the amount that even the most generous of newspapers will offer. And I'll make her sign a legal document promising not to go to the papers. Ever."

"OK, that might work," Gareth said, still rubbing his throat.

"It will work."

"How can you be so sure?"

"Trust me, it won't be the first time I've had some young tart paid off. Now, grab her ankles and help me carry her to my car."

Gareth did as he was told, and two minutes later Nick was screaming out of the drive, the girl laid across his back seat.

He floored it along the country road Gareth's mansion was on. Three of his other clients lived on the same road, so he knew the twists and turns well. Within minutes he was pulling over to the side of a city-centre back road, one where he knew there was no CCTV. He left her slumped against a wall and headed back towards Gareth's, calling for an ambulance as he did so.

And this was how Nick made his living. Or part of it anyway. Sometimes it was easier than this. Fifty percent of his work was advising his wealthy-client list on how to keep their homes and persons secure. He advised them on which security systems to install, he taught them how to keep themselves and their loved ones safe. If necessary, he would teach them or their WAGS self-defence techniques. His client list included judges, footballers, bankers, soap stars and pop stars. Most of them, directly or indirectly, introduced to him by Michael Epson. The other fifty percent of his workload was shit like this. And, of course, the clients that asked him to do things like this were the ones that paid the best. This is how he paid for the house, the cars and the clothes, by being permanently on call to these people, to drag people out of the shit. Shit that was usually of their own making.

He turned back onto Gareth's driveway, this time driving calmly. As he pulled up to the house, Gareth was sitting on the front steps, anxiously running his fingers through his hair. He stood up as Nick got out of his car.

"Well, what happened?"

"Exactly what I said would happen."

"So she's alive then?"

"She was when I left her."

"Fucking hell, Nick, this isn't funny."

"Who's joking? She was alive when I left her, and I'm sure she is now. I'll go and visit her in hospital and make a deal with her. I'll call you when I figure out how much it's gonna cost you."

Gareth sat back down on the step.

"Thanks, Nick, you're a fucking lifesaver."

"No problem. And next time you pick up some young skank, make sure she's not fucking diabetic."

*

Nick closed the gate of the storage facility and locked it. He glanced up at the CCTV cameras, and felt reassured by their presence as he slowly drove his car past the rows and rows of units. There were so many of them here, it was like a mini-city. His unit was almost at the very back. He unlocked the metal door and slid it noisily up. He switched the light on and stuck his head back outside to make sure nobody was around. He minimised the possibility of ever bumping into anyone by also renting the units on either side of this one. He slid the metal back down and locked it from inside. Only now did he feel secure. The room was almost bare. In one corner there was a small table with a single chair. On the table was an old photo album. Inside there were pictures of only his mother and himself. In the opposite corner was the thing that warranted all this security and secrecy. Bolted to the floor was a Phoenix Castille 0602E safe. The 0602E wasn't a huge safe by any means, measuring only 620mm in height and 460mm in depth, but it was a model that came highly recommended. It provided up to eight six-digit security codes, three 30mm-thick sliding bolts and a unique barrier design that provided extra protection against drilling. Nick punched in the three separate security codes then slid the bolts across and slowly opened the door. The adjustable shelf was situated almost at the bottom of the safe. This was necessary to accommodate the growing stash of cash he kept in there. He added the money he had taken from Francis to it. He now had well over a hundred grand in there. He kept it there in case of an emergency. He was never sure what kind of emergency would ever call for that kind of money, but he had to know it was here. He had money in high-yield fixed bonds, some in an off-shore account, he had some in accessible savings accounts, but he felt the need to keep this stash here. Lisa had no idea this place existed. He patted the money and moved his hand to the bottom of the safe and took out the bag. He opened it up and gripped the item that he really came here to look at. He took out the second-generation Glock 17 pistol. It was a Norwegian army issue, and had found its way into his hands via some gangland contacts he'd made while he was still on the force. He held it and aimed at the wall. He slid a round into the chamber. The G17 was one of the most reliable handguns on the market. Nick turned the gun around and slid the barrel into his mouth. He bit down on it, nearly gagging on the barrel, the oily taste turning his stomach. He placed his thumb on the trigger and pressed down lightly, stopping just short of the pressure needed to fire it. He knew just the tiniest bit more pressure now and the back of his head would be blown out, leaving his brains all over the wall and floor. Nobody in his life knew about this place. He was locked in, and the thickness of the walls would probably ensure the shot wouldn't be heard. He could lie here for days, weeks, months, maybe even longer, without being discovered. He took his thumb off the trigger, placed the gun back in the safe and locked it.

SIX

Scott gripped his right thigh and flexed the muscle there; absolutely rock solid. That whole morning in the gym had been dedicated to his legs. A solid forty minutes on the leg press, pushing well over a hundred kilos, followed by the same amount of time on the leg curl. He was very disciplined when it came to leg days. A lot of the other lads neglected their legs, giving a cursory twenty or thirty reps session, all of them focussing on their pecs and arms. Scott never fell into that trap. He just made sure he spent one day extra in the gym each week to sculpt his legs. There was no point having broad shoulders and a big chest if you were gonna have spindly fucking legs. Kev and Jimmy were there today too, and the extra work he'd been putting in lately was beginning to tell. In the showers afterwards he was able to notice how much better he was looking than the pair of them. They were all roughly the same size, but Scott was much more toned. Kev's shoulders were lacking, Jimmy needed to pump his pecs a bit more, and they both neglected their legs. They both looked good, but Scott looked better. Much better. The tight white T-shirt he wore now accentuated his upper-body muscularity. He wore it just for that reason, and in the hope that Carrie would notice and be impressed. If he was looking good, that was only gonna increase his chances of winning her back. Good first impressions. They were important.

There she was, coming in through the door now. She was looking beautiful, as always. Some women needed a ton of makeup to look their best. Carrie barely needed any, she was that much of a natural beauty. She scanned the café. He didn't try to attract her attention, he was enjoying watching her too much to interrupt it now. Eventually her eyes met his. He smiled and waved to her. Only a half-smile crept across her face. That was a good sign. She was clearly keeping her cards close to her chest, not wanting to give much away, but she still couldn't prevent just that little bit of a smile cracking. He felt his chances go up by ten percent or so. He stood up to greet her as she reached the table. He leaned in to give her a kiss on the cheek. She held back from him a little. He felt like a fucking idiot for trying that, but was relieved that she accepted his embrace, if not the kiss.

"I've got you a latte in, that alright?"

"Yeah that's fine, thanks."

"No problem. So, how are things?"

"OK, you know. Nothing special to report."

"Your mam and dad OK?"

"Yeah, they're good. In fact, Dad said to say hello from him."

Scott smiled. He had always got on well with Karl, Carrie's dad. More so than with her mum. She had always been a bit suspicious of him. He had sensed it from the first time he'd met her. That way she had of looking at him, like she was sizing him up, sussing him out. As though she had already made her mind up about him before she had even set eyes on him, and was just looking for something to confirm her thoughts. Miserable old cunt. Karl was alright, though. Karl was sound. Never gave him any problems, and always seemed glad to see him. He assumed Carrie mustn't have told Karl about what happened. He wouldn't be sending greetings if he knew what he'd done.

"So, what did you wanna say to me, Scott?"

Scott leaned back in his chair and took a deep breath.

"Well, first of all... I just wanna say sorry again for what I did. I know there's absolutely no excuse for it. I was bang out of order. I know no man should ever hit a woman, but I just lost control for a minute, not even that, just a second really. And it won't ever happen again. If you give me another chance, I swear I will never raise my hand to you again, babes. Never."

Carrie wiped a tear away from her face.

"That's what men always say when they've hit their

35

girl, isn't it? They all say it was a one-off, that it won't happen again, how sorry they are. Then they *do* do it again. I don't wanna be one of these woman that go back to a fella after they've hit them. I don't wanna be like that."

"I know that, and I know I've let you down. But I'm not like that. I'm not one of those men. I'm not a woman-beater. I lost control just for a split second, but I won't ever let that happen again. Never. I swear to you, Carrie. Please, just let me prove myself to you. I'll prove to you how good a man I can be. And I know I won't let you down again, coz I'm a better man when I'm with you. I... I love you, Carrie. You know that."

"I love you too," she said, and Scott thought his heart might just explode with joy. "But I'm not gonna take you back just like that. You have to prove yourself to me first, then we'll talk about us getting back together."

"That's fair. I will win you back, Carrie. I promise you."

Carrie wiped away some more tears with her sleeve.

"And I want you to promise me something else."

"Anything."

"I want you to stop using the steroids. Your temper's so much worse when you're using them. I mean it, Scott. If you don't pack them in, then we're finished. For good."

"I've already stopped taking them," he lied. Just that morning he had taken some Anadrol 50, and yesterday some Cypionate. "I don't touch them anymore. Never will do again. I'll give them up for good for you, I promise."

SEVEN

"... so what was the author trying to tell us? What is the *sub*text of this passage? Anyone?"

Chris stared out of the window at the building site across the road. It was blazing hot out there today, so most of the fellas on the site had their shirts off.

"Anybody at all?"

Chris couldn't stop looking at one of them. He was bald, about thirty-five or forty – Chris could never tell that accurately with older ones. He was broad-shouldered, muscular and tattooed. Chris realised he was developing *a type*. He hadn't so much as kissed a man, but already he was developing a type. He turned away from the window. He looked around him at his class. Or at the girls anyway. His English Lit class was full of them. Pretty teen girls with tight bodies, perky little tits and that unmistakable smell that teen girls gave off. It was, quite simply, the smell of pussy. And a boy of Chris's age, as good looking as he was, should have been in his element. But they did nothing for him. No girls did, not the ones in his class, not the ones that hung around outside the offie offering him a nosh if he got some booze for them. Not the ones he saw out in the Krazy House rock club. He'd tried as well. He'd copped off with plenty of the rock chicks, after he'd drunk enough pints of cheap beer and done enough speed. A couple of times he'd even gone home with them and fucked them. They seemed to enjoy it, and always went after him again when he next saw them out, but he knew one fuck was the most he was gonna be capable of with them. So he'd managed to earn himself a rep as a bit of a use-them-then-lose-them player, which just made the girls even keener on him. There was hardly a girl in the Krazy House he hadn't at least had a snog and grope session with.

"Mr McGann… Chris?"

Chris had no idea how long Tim, his English lecturer, had been talking to him.

"Sorry, Tim," he said, finally shifting his attention away from the builder. "I was miles away."

"So I see. Any ideas you'd like to share with us? What was the writer talking about?"

"Sex."

A few of his classmates giggled. A couple of the girls looked round at him.

"OK. Care to elaborate at all?"

Chris turned back to the building site as he continued. "It's about sex."

The builder stopped and wiped his brow. His muscles tightened as he did so.

"That's all anything is about. Sex. Fucking."

He turned back to the rest of his class. Now every girl in the room was staring at him. He could see the desire in their eyes, every one of them. He knew his already massive sexual cachet had just increased exponentially with that one remark. The only thing coming close to matching the sexual tension he had just created in the room was the seething resentment he had just fostered from all the other lads in the class. Not that he really gave a fuck about that.

"Right," his teacher said. "Thank you for that very blunt piece of insight, Mr McGann."

He turned back to the text, and Chris leaned back in his chair and turned his head back to the builder.

EIGHT

The Cedar Nursing Home was housed in a nineteenth-century structure which had been converted and extended in 1993 to house thirty-two self-contained flats, in which residents (never had the word *patients* been used at Cedar) were encouraged to live as independently as possible, as far as safely permissible, with varying levels of support, all tailored to fit the individual resident's needs. From twenty-four hour one-to-one support, to support activated only through emergency alarms, everybody, of every possible need, was catered for. As well as the Victorian building structure, Cedar also boasted opulent grounds, nearly two acres, which residents were free to use at their leisure.

In the Cedar car park, Nick gripped the steering wheel of his Evoque. He pressed his head against the wheel, willing himself to open the door and get the fuck out. He took his right hand off the wheel and grabbed the door handle. His knuckles turned white as he gripped the latch. He tasted bile. He swallowed it back down and gulped in a deep breath and shoved the door open. He tried to regulate his breathing. Seven seconds breathing in, followed by eleven seconds breathing out, just as the last therapist he had been to had advised him. He literally grabbed his own right leg in both hands and lifted his foot up, placing it down on the asphalt of the Cedar car park. This time he couldn't keep the bile down. He retched and puked on the concrete right next to his foot, a few drops of vomit shrapnel splattering on his shoe. He retracted his foot and slammed the door shut. He slammed his head against the steering wheel, an inappropriately comical, accidental hoot of the horn sounding out. He opened the glove box and took out his hip flask. He unscrewed it and took a generous gulp of the bourbon inside. He grabbed the bag of coke from the glove box and clumsily lined up a line on the dashboard, losing half the contents of the bag as he did so. He snorted it and quickly lined up and did another line. Another slug of bourbon while he waited for the beak to kick in. Some slow breathing exercises took the edge off the shakes, the burning glow from the bourbon spread through him, and he felt the coke finally take effect. He took a deep breath and pushed the car door open and got out determinedly. Without hesitation he walked into Cedar. He nodded to the staff at the nurses' station and walked through the main lounge area. It was the usual depressing site, a group of residents staring at the horse racing on the television, others scattered around the room in the big chairs, some of them sleeping. It never failed to turn his stomach to see these old fools dribbling on themselves as they slept away what remained of their pathetic lives, stinking of piss or shit. This may be the best nursing home in the area, but there was only so much they could do, and even the best-cared-for old people still stank the same. He walked quickly through the lounge area – he knew his dad wouldn't be there, he shunned the company of most of the shut-ins, spending most of his time in his flat. As he reached his flat he hovered just out of sight outside the open door. He could hear his dad's voice, and that of another man. He peeked through the door and saw his dad, sitting in the big comfy chair as one of the young male staff perched on the edge of the bed. Nick's dad had him almost doubled over as he recounted some story or other from his youth. John Hanman, every bit the bon viveur and raconteur. The staff here loved him, his sense of humour and independence barely dimmed, despite the two strokes he had had in the last five years. The only real legacy of the strokes seemed to be reduced mobility, particularly down his left side, but he still got about mostly unaided and his mental faculties remained intact.

"Anyway, John, I'll leave you to it," the young man said as he stood up.

"Aye, alright then, lad, you go and attend to your duties and I'll see you later."

Nick walked into the room just as he left, receiving a friendly hello. John looked up as Nick entered.

"Ah, it's my only son."

"Alright, Dad," Nick said, shaking his dad's hand. John gave him the usual bone-cruncher. He kept hold of Nick's hand a few beats longer than necessary. He looked his son in the eye. Nick was able to hold John's gaze only a few seconds before he had to look down at the floor. John finally let go of his hand. Nick turned away. He began to lower himself onto the bed, but changed his mind and hovered awkwardly instead.

"Why don't you sit yourself down, son?"

"No, it's OK," Nick said without making eye contact.

"Not staying long?"

"No, not really."

"No, you never fucking do, do you, son?"

Nick said nothing. He wandered over to the window and looked out at the gardens. His dad's flat had probably the best view of them, and a patio-style door that opened right onto them.

"Sit down."

"No, it's OK."

"I said sit the fuck down, son."

Nick felt the bile rise back up again. He didn't answer, but he walked back over to the bed and lowered himself down onto the corner that the staff had vacated.

"There, that's better, isn't it?"

Nick nodded his head.

"I said isn't it?"

"Yes, Dad."

"'Yes, Dad'," John said, mimicking the weak tone in his son's voice. "So have you got anything to say for yourself, or are you gonna just sit there like a fucking little nancy boy?"

"No."

"No, what? No, you haven't got anything to say for yourself or no, you're not gonna sit there like some fucking nancy?"

Nick's voice cracked as he spoke.

"No, I'm not gonna sit here."

"Like a....?"

"Like a nancy boy."

"Good."

John turned to the window and shook his head.

"I don't know where I went wrong with you, Nick. Although it's probably down to your mother that you turned out the way you did. She always molly-coddled you. The stupid cunt."

"Please don't call her that."

"You telling me what to do, boy?"

"No, I'm not," Nick's voice creaked again as he spoke, "I just..."

"You just what? Spit it out."

"I'd just rather you didn't talk about her like that."

He would rather he didn't talk about her at all. To hear him talk about her in any capacity felt to Nick like John was pissing on her grave.

"I'll talk about whoever I please, however I please. I don't need your fucking approval. You hear?"

"Sorry."

"That's better. Now, what have you got for your old dad today?"

John pointed at the plastic bag in Nick's hand. Nick reached inside it and pulled out a tall, thin, cardboard box.

"Ooh, is that what I think it is?" John asked, his demeanour suddenly changing.

"Yes, I believe it probably is," Nick replied, holding out the box.

"Lagavulin Single Malt Scotch Whiskey," John said, squinting to read the elaborate font on the box. "Very nice, son, very fucking nice indeed."

Nick stood up and presented the box to him, like a waiter in a posh restaurant displaying a bottle of fine wine. *Et voila.* John took it from him as though it were a piece of delicate bone china.

"I'll say one thing for you, son, you always pick the good stuff. There's a couple of glasses over on the table there.

Bring them over."

Nick walked over to the table and picked up the glasses. He rinsed them in the sink in the en-suite bathroom as his father continued to read from the box.

"'Lagavulin Distillery, Port Ellen, Isle of Islay. Aged twelve years'. Twelve years, son." He opened the box and slid the bottle out and beheld its beauty. He unscrewed the cap and held the bottle to his nose. "Mmmm, that smell. Nice and peaty, with a hint of tobacco. Absolutely fucking beautiful."

Nick brought the glasses over and John poured a large measure into them. John took a tiny sip, barely wetting his lips, while Nick knocked his straight back.

"Don't just belt it like that, for fuck's sake, don't be such a fucking philistine," his dad said, instantly pouring Nick another. "It's not a glass of fucking Jack Daniels or whatever shite it is you drink. This is the good stuff. Savour it, let it drop slowly down, let yourself feel the warmth as it goes down."

Nick did as instructed this time, feeling the burn as he swallowed. He felt the first shot mixing with the bourbon and cocaine already in his system. He felt the need inside. Drink or drugs were the usual triggers, as was visiting his dad. All three factors combined meant the need was impossible to ignore.

"Listen, Dad, I'm gonna have to get going."

"Oh, what a fucking surprise. You've barely been here five fucking minutes."

"I know, I'm sorry."

"What is it? Work or family?"

"Work. I've just got some things to sort out. And family too after that."

"Well that's not so bad then. Family's important, son. There's nothing more important than family. Remember that."

"I will, Dad, I'll see you soon."

Nick offered his hand for shaking. John took it in his vice-like grip and held it for half a minute, his grip tightening by the second. He finally released it.

"Bye, son, and bring my grandchild with you next time."

"Bye, Dad."

Nick left the room and walked back through the lounge. He quickened his pace, desperate to get back out to the safety of his car. A coffin-dodger stepped in front of him.

"When do I get my pills?" he asked.

"Fuck off, you old cunt," Nick snarled in his face, nearly knocking him down as he barged past him. He quickened his pace further as he walked through the front door. As soon as he got into the car park he broke into a sprint back to his car. He fumbled his keys as he tried desperately to get inside it, now feeling almost as though his life depended on him finding refuge there. He slammed the door shut behind him as he got in. He gripped the steering wheel tight as he burst into tears. He opened the glove box and took the bag of coke back out. His hands were shaking uncontrollably, so instead of cutting a line he stuck his nose inside like a horse in a feedbag and sucked up as much as he could. He snorted again then withdrew his nose from the bag. He opened his flask and thirstily glugged down what was left. The warmth spread through his body, the booze and the drugs now all starting to work. He breathed slowly till he felt he had control of his hands again. He turned the key in the ignition and reversed out of the car park, and headed towards Sally's.

"Who is it?" Sally's voice came through the intercom almost as soon as Nick pressed the buzzer.

"It's Nick. Are you busy?"

"Never too busy for you, darling. Come on in."

She buzzed him in, and Nick pushed open the thick mahogany door. He let it slam shut behind him.

"In the kitchen."

Nick followed the sound of the voice at the end of the hallway. Sally was standing at the sink with her back to him.

"Cup of tea?" she asked without turning round.

"Fuck, yes. Love one."

Nick took a seat at the kitchen table and picked up a block of weed there, and began skinning up.

"How's tricks?" Nick almost shouted over the sound of the kettle.

"Is that a deliberate play on words?"

"No, just a figure of speech."

"Well, what's the line from that Talking Heads song? 'Same as it ever was'."

Sally placed the mug of tea on the table and sat down.

"Right. Nuff said."

Nick finished rolling the spliff and lit it up, taking in a huge lungful. He'd never been a big pothead but he wasn't averse to it and, feeling as frazzled as he currently was, it was just what he needed. He took another monster drag and passed it to Sally.

"Thanks, love," she said, accepting it and instantly taking a large draw of her own. "Fucking hell," she said coughing, "that's a bit fucking strong, innit? Even for you."

Nick turned to face her, laughing.

"Nah, you're just a fucking lightweight, Sal. Hang on, what the fuck is that?"

He held her chin in his hand and turned her face slightly. There was the start of what would eventually become a pretty impressive shiner underneath her left eye.

"What cunt gave you that?"

"Who do you think? A client."

"A regular?"

"Yeah, he's pretty regular."

"Fucking bastard. Who is he?"

"Why? You gonna go round to his house and batter him for me?"

"You're fucking right I am."

"Oh, so you're the grizzled ex-copper taking care of the tart with a heart? That's a bit fucking clichéd for you, isn't it?"

"You think it's funny?"

"No. I don't think it's fucking funny, Nick. But it happens. It's not that big a deal."

"Someone giving you a fucking great big black eye isn't a big deal?"

"For fuck's sake, Nick. I've had worse, believe me. It's an occupational hazard. Sometimes men just get a bit carried away, that's all. This one's not a bad guy."

"There's no fucking excuse for that shit."

"Look, forget it. Just think of it this way: a man's got extreme tastes or urges or what have you, maybe it's better that he comes here and takes it out on me a bit than carry that round with him. If he didn't let it out with me in this... controlled environment, you might say, then he might be taking some poor young thing off the streets and doing a lot worse to her. I'm performing a public service. Giving something back to society."

"Stop fucking joking about it. It's not funny."

"Here," she said, handing him the spliff back. "Just smoke some more of this and unclench your fists. You didn't come here to talk about some other punter of mine, did you?"

Nick took another toke.

"No."

"Shall we go downstairs?"

Nick breathed slowly out through his nostrils, engulfing himself in smoke. He nodded his head.

*

In the basement. Nick, naked, kneeled down on the concrete floor, scraping his knees. He felt the collar go round his neck.

"Tighter," he said. Sally tightened it. He felt the leash being clipped onto the collar. He heard the other end of it being clipped onto the metal bracket on the wall. Sally handcuffed his hands behind his back. He leaned forward, feeling the collar tighten as he did so. Sally took his cock in her hand and started slowly massaging it. He felt himself getting hard. He pushed his top half further forward. Around his neck, the collar tightened more. Sally wanked him harder, with big, long pumps of her fist. He leaned even further forward, the leash tightening. He let the top half of his body slump forward completely. The leash tightened, and he felt weightless as he leaned into mid-air. It almost felt as if he was flying. They called this hangman. Sally knew to wank him harder now.

"Say it," he managed to croak.

"You dirty little bastard," she said. "You vile, pathetic

fucking pig. You fucking lowly little maggot. You fucking disgust me."

"More."

"You fucking worthless little nancy boy. You fucking vile little faggot. Freak. Filthy little freak. You're fucking grotesque. Ugly, scarred bastard."

*

Sally charged ninety-five pounds an hour. Not one hundred. She kept her prices as low as she could, always trying to undercut the competition, as well as being willing to do a lot of stuff the others wouldn't. An exclusive service, offered at a competitive price. That was capitalism in a nutshell, Nick supposed. Nick was there for a little over half that time, but he gave her the best part of two hundred, like he always did. As Nick reached the front door, he stopped.

"If that client hits you again, I'll fucking kill him. I mean it."

Sally sighed.

"My hero," she said sarcastically.

He let himself out.

NINE

Scott watched Kev carry the lads' bevvies over and place them clumsily down on the table. Kev had been neglecting his workout regime this last week or so. His upper arms were lacking definition. His forearms still had great tone, Scott would give him that, but he was getting lazy. There was no other word for it. Scott felt like picking up one of the pint glasses and grinding it into his fucking face. He couldn't stand people slacking off when it came to their physique. Made him sick.

Pale lager spilled from the tops of the glasses and formed a mini-river that snaked its way towards Scott, the tip of it trickling over the edge of the table and onto his jeans.

"Fuck's sake, Kev," he said, standing up and wiping his jeans down with his hand.

"Alright, take it easy," Kev said, dropping a few beer mats on top of the river of lager to try and soak some of it up.

"Don't fucking tell me to take it easy, look at the state of me fucking jeans now."

"Oh it's only a little fucking splash, mate," Marty said.

"Yeah," Kev agreed. "Just dry them off under the hand-dryer in the bogs."

Scott pointed his finger inches from Kev's face.

"Don't fucking tell me what to do. And you," he moved his finger to Marty's face. "You mind your own fucking business."

"Fucking hell, mate. I didn't mean nothing by it."

Scott sat back down. His mood swings were getting worse. He knew it was the 'roids. He thought about what he had promised Carrie. He knew he was going to have to get it under control sooner or later, but he was too into his current

48

fitness routine, and the steroids were an integral part of that. He needed to keep hitting them for a few more weeks, just till he got his body how he wanted it to look, then he could think about reducing the steroid intake and increasing his workouts accordingly. He sat back down; he was about to apologise to the lads for his outburst but then he noticed Kev and Marty exchanging a look. He saw something in their eyes and he knew instantly what it was. It was fear. He had scared them. Looking the way he did, Scott was not new to the sensation of causing someone fear. Working on nightclub doors, it was sort of part of the job. But he had never seen Kev or Marty react to him like that, and he very much liked how it made him feel.

"Here's a good one," Marty said in an attempt to lighten the mood. "What do you call ten thousand dead Pakis?"

But Scott wasn't listening. He was looking past Kev and Marty at the door of the pub. As he was looking, he saw a man walk in and look around. He took a few more steps in and was scanning the pub, trying to locate someone. He looked in Scott's direction and smiled with recognition. Scott wondered who he was and why he was looking at him. Did he know him? From where? The gym? Possibly. The tight, black T-shirt the man was wearing showed that he had good muscular definition, albeit contained within a thin overall frame. It was definitely a gym physique, but more closely resembled the preening faggots than Scott and his mates. So why the fuck was this man staring at him now? He began walking towards Scott, now smiling broadly at him. The rest of the pub seemed to melt away, the sounds reduced to a low, bassy thrum, as Scott's eyes locked with this guy's. Scott felt himself become paralysed with fear. He looked at Kev and Marty to see if they were aware of his current plight, but they were too wrapped up in Marty's joke to notice. Scott wanted to stand up and run, or to throw this man through the fucking window. He gripped the wooden arms of his chair as the man reached his table. He felt the wood creaking as the man walked straight past Scott to the group of men at the table behind him. He stood up and without saying anything to his friends he walked hurriedly to the toilet.

He locked himself in the cubicle and breathed deeply. What the fuck was that? What the fuck had just happened. He breathed deeply till he calmed down. He reached into his pocket and took out the little plastic bag. He scooped a little bit of the powder out of there with the corner of his credit card and snorted it. He had never been a big coke user. Him and the boys did some from time to time, sometimes a bit of speed; it helped when you worked long and late hours like they did, gave you a bit of a boost. They'd do the odd tablet as well, but Scott always felt heavy drug usage was incompatible with his strict exercise regime. With all the stress of the last few weeks though, with everything that had been going on with Carrie, he had been doing it a bit more than usual. Just to help him relax. He walked to the sink and splashed some water on his face. He left the toilets and walked back to his table. The man in the black T-shirt was already engaged in conversation with three other men at his table. His instinct was right, these men were obviously queer. He sat back down with his back to them and gripped the arms of the chair again.

"You seen these fuckers?" Kev asked. Scott said nothing.

"Fucking queers. Look at them," Marty said. Scott turned his head slightly to the side so he could see them. "Fucking laughing and joking like it's nothing. As though it's fucking normal."

Scott's grip tightened on the arms of his chair. He could feel his heart punching him from inside his chest. A trickle of sweat ran down his back.

"Fucking sick, innit, Scott?" Kev asked. But Scott couldn't speak. He was paralysed again. "Scott?" The wood creaked in his hands. "I said isn't it, Scott?"

The wooden arms of the chair broke off in Scott's hands. The sound it made was like rifle fire, and almost everyone in the pub turned towards the source of the sound – a few people had even ducked slightly in an effort to dodge the bullet they thought they'd heard. Scott stood up, two splintered planks of wood in his hands.

"Fucking faggots," he shouted at the table behind him,

50

and stormed out of the pub.

*

Friday nights, Scott worked the doors at Liberty nightclub and bar with Kev and Marty, as well as a couple of other boys. Seven through till kicking-out time at three the next morning. They did a good job too. They had the right balance of firmness and fairness, and knew each other's strengths and weaknesses. A well-oiled machine, that's what they were. And there was a decent crowd of regulars there too. Obviously you got some troublemakers, lairy lads who had far too much to drink and thought they could take Scott or the others on. They needed to be put in their place quick-sharp, and Scott and the boys weren't afraid to use their fists when necessary, but they were also able to diffuse difficult situations before having to resort to firmer measures. They prided themselves on it, in fact. For the most part, though, it wasn't a bad crowd. And the birds. Well, they were the icing on the cake. One side-benefit of being a bouncer was that you were never short of pussy. There was a type of girl that just loved bouncers. That actively pursued them. And it wasn't usually the type of girl you'd expect. You might expect it to be skanky older ones, but it was in fact, more often than not, the sweetest-looking, prettiest girl-next-door type. Must have been the attraction of the bit of rough. Scott had lost count of the number of times he'd clocked some pretty young thing coming in with her boyfriend, and ended up getting sucked off by her in the toilets while the boy waited at the bar, blissfully unaware his missus was on her knees with a gob full of bouncer cock. Sometimes he felt bad about it. Doing it behind Carrie's back, he knew that was wrong. But he figured that, if she never knew about it, where was the harm? It wasn't like he loved these girls. He loved Carrie absolutely. She was his everything. No matter how many women he fucked or got sucked off by, he would always go back to Carrie. He'd never want any other woman waiting for him at the end of a hard night's work on the doors. Getting home at close to four in the morning, and sliding into their warm bed next to her... well, nothing beat that. And all the blow jobs and sports fucking in the world wouldn't change that.

It was getting close to midnight now, and the club was bouncing. Round about the midnight hour was the best part of the night. People had had enough drink to have loosened up, but not so much that they were getting too aggro, the crowd that were in were mostly in there for the duration rather than passing through. The DJ saved all the best tunes for this part of the night. The punters were dancing, they were nicely boozed up, or nicely pilled up, and they were horny. The buzz Scott got from this part of the night, it was what he loved about this job. Some nights, round this time, he wasn't averse to dropping the odd tab of E himself, just to really make it a good night. Tonight was one such night. Kev had brought a bag of Garries out with him, and Scott decided to drop three of them tonight, the pills kicking in beautifully just as the DJ put on some Robert Myles. He stood now, leaning against the pillar at the side of the dance floor, swigging from a bottle of water, feeling the ecstasy course through his body, watching the young bodies writhe to the music. The short skirts, the low-cut tops, the sexy high heels, so much young flesh glistening with sweat. This was what he needed to focus on. Those other thoughts he'd been having lately, he didn't know what they were all about, but it didn't matter as long as he was looking at all these girls, women, birds. This was what he needed right now. Now one of them was dancing right in front of him. Tight little mini-dress. Long, blonde hair. Perky young tits. Nice tight little arse. He thought for a split second about Carrie. But when such a sweet, fuckable young thing was offering it up on a fucking plate, how could he possibly refuse?

In the toilet cubicle, she stuck her tongue deep inside his mouth, pushing it against his. She moved his hands up to her tits and he squeezed them hard. She unzipped his trousers and pulled out his semi-hard cock.

"You like that?" she said as she wanked him hard. A bit too hard. Her grip was too tight. No matter, though. Her tongue was like silk, and he let her slide down onto her knees and take him in her mouth. She looked up at him with those pretty, blue eyes as she moved her mouth back and forth on his cock. She started sucking him harder. Again, it was a bit too hard, and he felt her teeth against the head of his cock. He took her hair in his hands and tried to slow her sucking down a bit. She took his cock out of her mouth and spat on it. She obviously thought this would turn him on but he just thought it was a bit gross. It was obviously something she'd seen on some porno, or something her boyfriend liked her to do, but it did fuck all for him. She obviously thought she was the ultimate cocksucker, but he realised she was just some young, dumb little tart who didn't know half as much as she though she did. He felt himself starting to soften a bit. He guided his cock back into her mouth and closed his eyes. He thought about naked flesh, tits, arses and wet pussies. It didn't work, he felt himself getting softer still. Then, from nowhere, in his mind's eye, a flash of the guy in the black T-shirt from the pub earlier. What the fuck? Where in fuck did that come from? He looked down at the gorgeous little slut sucking on his cock, but when she looked up at him, he realised she wasn't that gorgeous after all. She had pretty bad skin, which she had clearly attempted to cover up with layers of makeup, but all the sweat was making it run, the glare from the lights in the bogs acting like an X-ray through the makeup to the spots and blemishes underneath. He reached down and grabbed her tit but realised that she was wearing a padded bra, and was actually pretty flat-chested. He closed his eyes again, but instantly got a flash of the guy again. The tight T-shirt against his toned body. Scott shook his head to try and push the image out. He felt himself getting harder again, but the faggot wouldn't leave. As his cock got hard, he thought of the faggot with his boyfriend. He thought of them sucking each other's cocks, licking each other's arse holes. What the fuck was going on? Where the fuck had this come from? He looked down at the slut. He wrapped her hair around his hands and started to fuck her mouth hard. She gagged on his cock and tried to pull away. Scott tightened his grip on her hair and pushed her down on his now rock-hard cock. She tried to pull away but he wouldn't let her. He felt his orgasm rising up from his balls. Again, the naked body of the faggot flashed in his mind. He throat-fucked the little slut harder till he felt himself explode inside her mouth. He felt jet after jet of spunk flow into her. He finally let go of her and she instantly puked a mixture of come and bile into the toilet. He didn't stick around. He marched straight out of the cubicle, through the club and out to the boys on the door.

"Cover for me, lads, gotta shoot off," he shouted at them without slowing down. He ran round to his car and got in. He put his head on the steering wheel. He head-butted it, and again and again. He turned the key in the ignition and headed the fuck out of there.

TEN

Liverpool by night. There was nowhere quite like it. Over the other side of the city centre was the Krazy House rock club. Less than fifteen minutes on foot from Liberty, but it couldn't be more different. The shiny steel and polished glass motif of Liberty was a million miles away from the sticky floors, overflowing toilets and darkness of the Krazy House, one of the oldest and largest rock clubs in England. Three floors, each with its own dance floor and bar, as well as its own distinct clientèle; old-school rockers and bikers on the first floor, nu-metallers on the second, indie kids on the third. In a dark corner of the space between floors two and three, Chris and his friends occupied a booth. The table was filled with bottles of Budweiser and orange WKD and plastic pint glasses filled with varying amounts of lager, cider or combinations thereof. It was close to midnight, and things were clicking into gear, the cheap booze working its magic, the tunes were good and they were all sweaty from moshing to Rage Against The Machine on the second floor.

"Who's up for a bit of Billy Whizz?" Tommo asked, pulling a little plastic bag from the pocket of his jeans.

A chorus of affirmation rose at once from the table. Tommo dipped his finger into the bag, then stuck it in his mouth like he was eating sherbet. He passed the bag along and everyone took their turn. Chris snorted a little mountain of it off his little finger nail and took a swig of his snakebite to wash away the bitter aftertaste. He reached into his own pocket and produced a bag of pills.

"I'll see your bag of speed and raise you a bag of Es, good sir," he shouted over the odd blend of Linkin Park from the second floor and The Libertines coming down from the third.

"Sir, I accept your challenge," Tommo shouted back, opening his mouth.

Chris took a pill from the bag and, thinking only briefly how much he'd love to shove his cock in there, threw a perfectly aimed tablet into his friend's mouth. Chris put two tablets on his own tongue and knocked them back with another mouthful of snakebite and, just as Tommo had done, passed his wares around for his friends to share. Now it was time for some shots. Chris and Pete went to the bar and came back with a tray of tequilas, which everyone duly sank. Chris was about to suggest another round when the opening bars of Nirvana's "Drain You" rang out from downstairs.

"Oh, fucking classic tuuuuune!" Chris shouted. He didn't have to say anything else. His friends had all had the exact same thought as him, and they all sprinted to the dance floor and joined the undulating throng of people dancing. *"I don't care what you think unless it is about me"* they screamed in unison. A good-looking girl stared at Chris through the mass of bodies. Her brown eyes looked through her angular black fringe. *"It is now my duty to completely drain you"*. Chris stared back at her. *"I drive it through a tube..."* Chris felt the E and speed kicking right in. *"... chew meat for you..."* He walked to her through the crowd. She smiled as she saw him approaching. He didn't say anything to her, he just took her face in his hands and, with perfect Hollywood timing, kissed her as Kurt Cobain sang *"... pass a kiss, from my mouth to yours..."*.

In the toilets, Chris did another fat line of speed and dropped another couple of pills. Back on the dance floor, the brunette punk girl long since dispensed with, Chris let another girl dance up against him. She leaned into his ear and told him her name. He wasn't listening. His eyes rolled back in his head as he listened to Arctic Monkeys telling him he looked good on the dance floor, and he knew full well that he did.

Then he was down on the first floor, slamming to Biohazard with the hairy rockers. He slammed into one burly rocker, hoping he'd take the hint, drag him into the toilets and fuck him senseless. Instead he slammed his shoulder into

Chris's chest, sending him flying onto the filthy floor.

Outside, he shared a spliff with an old hippy who made him promise to check out some King Crimson. He stood alone and chained a few ciggies, revelling in the cold air of the Liverpool night. He leaned back against the cold brick wall as he sucked down the last of his ciggie, watching the crowds pass by, knowing in his heart that, happy as they all were, not one of them was having as good a night as he was.

Back on the top floor, he found his mates all standing with their arms round each other's shoulders, singing Oasis's 'Wonderwall'. They were taking the piss. Every one of his mates hated Oasis with a passion. He pushed his way into the circle and sang at the top of his voice with the rest of them. Some pissed-up old scally tried to join them, and they parted to allow him access. He bellowed the words passionately and tunelessly. He didn't know they were taking the piss, but it didn't matter. They were buzzing off him anyway. As the song ended, the scally bought them a round of drinks and kissed them all on the lips before he headed home.

Leaning against the pool table, his hands on the arse of yet another girl, the last of the pills and speed done, he realised something. He had to fuck someone tonight. He had been walking round with a hard-on half the night, the E and the raging speed-horn combining to make him one horny little bastard. Somebody was gonna get fucked tonight, and, while he knew it wasn't what he was really after, this girl was gonna have to do for now.

Back at her place, he pulled her knickers down and spread her legs wide apart. He put his mouth on her wet cunt and licked, because he knew it was what was expected of him. This is what young lads did. She grinded herself against his mouth, running her fingers through his hair as he licked her clit. The taste of her made him want to retch, but he kept going. The speed ensured he'd have no trouble staying hard for her. He turned her over and pulled out his cock. He pressed it against the lips of her cunt and pushed himself inside her. He closed his eyes and thought of the builder he'd seen through the window of his classroom. He thought about his shaven head and his muscles. He pumped away at the stupid little girl, who screamed with pleasure. As always, when he had taken E, it took him forever to come. He knew this would make him appear even more of a badass, the stud who could keep going all night.

In his own bed afterwards, still hard, the raging speed-horn showed no signs of abating. He lay on his back, again his thoughts turning to the builder. The burly, muscular, nasty-looking builder. He thought about what he might do to him. He thought about being used roughly, fucked hard up his tight, little, teen arse, being made to suck the builder's hard cock until he filled his mouth with come. He came harder than he had with the girl. He cleaned the come off his belly and saw himself in the mirror. He crawled towards his reflection and put his face right up to the glass.

"You fucking dirty, little queer," he whispered.

ELEVEN

Hanman Total Security Solutions' office was situated on the third floor of an office building smack in the middle of Liverpool city centre. The Epson Complex was built eight years ago and HTSS was the first company to take up residence. It now shared space with ad agencies, accountants and law firms. The complex boasted private underground parking, twenty-four-hour security, a shop, coffee outlets and a restaurant on the ground floor. The surroundings were opulent, more so than a company the size of HTSS needed, but Nick loved the trappings that came with it, and the location was perfect. It was right in the heart of the city, and Nick felt plugged right into it. It was also roughly equidistant from his clients on the Wirral and those in Cheshire. The luxury came at a high price to all residents of Epson Complex, but the high-class client list ensured a steady influx of income that could comfortably cover it. Besides which, Nick had a guarantor.

"Morning, Nick," Kathleen said as he entered the office. Kathleen had been with the company since its inception. She was somewhere between a secretary, an office manager and a PA, and took care of the day-to-day running of the office. More than that, though, she took care of Nick. Although she was never fully aware of the extent of them, she was familiar with Nick's drink and drug habits, as well as many of his other shortcomings. Over the years, her efficiency had become crucial to the running of the firm and her no-bullshit approach to Nick had also become essential.

"Morning, Kathleen. So what's new today?"

"Nothing much. A few clients' contracts are up for renewal, so you'll need to give them a call and schmooze them a bit."

"You mean employ my charm and rapier wit to ensure they stay with our firm rather than go to one of our competitors?"

"That's about the size of it, yes. Oh, and Michael Epson called a couple of times."

"No problem, I'll pop up and see him in a few minutes."

Nick walked through to his own office and closed the door. He sat down at his desk and opened the draw. He took out a packet of diazepam. He popped out six milligrams' worth of tablets and knocked them back dry. He took a deep breath and walked out to the lift. He got in and pushed the button to take him up to the headquarters of Epson Enterprises Ltd. The company occupied the entire top floor, just three floors above HTSS. From the layout, Nick had worked out the Epson's own office was more or less directly above where Nick's was. As the lift doors closed behind him and the lift began its ascent, Nick stared at his reflection and took some deep breaths. He had known Michael Epson for the best part of twenty years, but each time Nick was summonsed – and it did feel like a summons, their relationship not quite extending to what one could call friendship but something much more complex than that – to see him, he felt the nervousness and fear of an errant schoolboy being called to the headmaster's office.

The lift opened onto the bustle of Epson Enterprises Ltd. Nick stepped out and bid the receptionist good morning. By now, she didn't have to ask if Nick had an appointment. Only if Epson was already in a meeting did Nick have to wait. This morning, he was ushered through and headed straight into his office.

"Nick, come in, close the door."

"Morning, Michael," Nick said as he sat down on the other side of the huge desk. "How are you?"

"Busier than a Jap prisoner of war, as always. Business is booming, I barely have the time to stop, lately."

"You wouldn't have it any other way though, would you now?"

"Ah, how well he knows me. Indeed, this is just the way I like it. But tell me, Nick, how are *you*?"

"Also busy, as usual."

"All those clients I helped find for you working you too hard, eh?"

There it was, the constant reminder of what Michael had done for him. Barely a conversation passed by without him dropping one in.

"Not *too* hard, but hard enough."

"Good. I think it's important for you to keep as busy as possible, Nick. Too much time to think draws you down the path of temptation, and allows some of your... shall we say baser instincts to take hold."

"Yes, I think you're right."

As Nick said this, he balled his fist inside his pockets. He could stand doing Epson's dirty work for him, he could stand all the murky business he was party to, but what he deeply resented was when Epson took that fatherly tone with him, and it made him want to punch his fucking lights out.

1996, Liverpool. Nick, then a sprog on the force, and high on crack, kicked open the door of a hotel room when the occupants wouldn't answer the door. Complaints had been made to the front desk about the loud music coming from room 228. The staff had been unable to gain access as the key was in the lock on the other side of the door, so the police had been called. Responding, Nick had knocked once and, when he received no answer, instantly put his foot to the door. On the third kick it swung open and Nick had entered to find a thirty-five-year-old Michael Epson with his mouth around the cock of a boy who couldn't have been more than fourteen years old. Nick didn't recognise him straight away, but even if he had, he still would have taken out his truncheon and slammed it into Epson's face. Epson went down, coughing up blood and a couple of teeth. Nick kicked him in the stomach and knelt astride his chest, grabbing him round the throat.

"Don't you know who I am?" Epson managed to choke out.

Nick then realised who he was looking at. Already one

of the wealthiest and most recognisable people on Merseyside. Before Nick had decided what he was going to do with him, a desperate and terrified Michael Epson managed to put forward an offer. A deal. Thinking quickly, he offered to do much more than pay Nick off. Sensing the moral flexibility he had become familiar with through the world of business, he had offered to become Nick's patron. To start with, he offered Nick the chance to moonlight as his personal security consultant, for which he would receive a sum that far exceeded his policeman's salary for doing very little actual work. Nick didn't even hesitate in accepting. There and then, he sold his soul, not to the devil but to Michael Epson. His work for Epson commenced immediately with the boy being paid off and things being smoothed over with the hotel. From then on, Nick continued his police career, but with a view to very little in the way of career advancement, knowing as he did that Epson was already more than doubling his salary, and, when he took early retirement from the force ten years ago, Epson had set Nick up in business as a full-time private security consultant. Not only did he pay the rent on Nick's office for as long as the company was active, he had provided Nick with a number of wealthy clients, putting a good word in for him with just about every wealthy or powerful person he came into contact with. Overnight, HTSS was set up with over twenty clients, to whom Nick offered security advice as well as being on call twenty-four hours a day. From there, Nick was able to put the few skills and contacts he had developed whilst on the force to good use and had become a fixer and trouble-shooter to his clients. Nick's discretion and ask-no-questions methods had led to lots of word-of-mouth work, often doing the kind of jobs only somebody who was willing to occasionally work outside the law would be capable of. Nick's efficiency with these more ad-hoc, one-off jobs usually led to repeat custom from the same clients. And always there, in the background, was Michael Epson, Nick's greatest benefactor. Thanks to him paying Nick's office rent, as well as the generous retainer he paid to have Nick always available to him, Nick could make a good living from the Epson account alone, but early on, Nick knew he wanted more than that, and Lisa, then just his girlfriend, wanted more, and encouraged him to network and build his list of clients as much as he could. Nick, knowing he had little to offer Lisa other than the comfort his income would bring, threw himself body and soul into his work. Thanks to his dedication, Nick was himself now a wealthy man. And employing only Kathleen full-time, as well as a couple of guys he used as and when he needed some extra help, which was very rarely, he had very few people he had to share his proceeds with.

"So. That little matter I asked you to take care of. Did things go as we hoped?"

"They did."

Nick got a flash of Francis's face through the plastic bag.

"And there won't be any repercussions from it?"

"No. We can be very confident of that."

A flash of Francis naked, face-down on the bed.

Michael leant forward onto his desk, his head resting on his hands.

"That's excellent news. I knew I could count on you, Nick. And how's the family?"

"They're fine, thanks."

"Monica. She must be... what? Three now?"

"Four."

"Wow. Four. Where does the time go? I'd love to meet her and Lisa sometime."

"Yeah, that'd be great."

No, it fucking wouldn't. Nick had gone to great lengths to ensure Michael had never met his young family. He wanted that to remain the one part of his life that was untouched by what he did for a living. The one area of purity in his life. He knew he was failing in that more and more.

"Then we must arrange it soon."

"Definitely."

"Alright, then. Good to catch up with you, Nick. Now, don't let me keep you. There's a big city out there, and a lot of money to be made in it."

TWELVE

Thirty kilos wasn't enough. It had been for a while, he had got results with it, but now he needed to push on. To take it up a notch. He put the dumbbell back on the rack and picked up the forty kilo weights, one in each hand. That was more like it. This is serious shit now. He sat on the bench and began doing seated lateral raises. He decided to start off with twenty, but when he got to that he kept going, aiming for fifty. But at fifty he just kept going again. When he reached seventy-five he had to stop, but instead of letting his arms drop he held them up and counted to ten before gently lowering them. He always liked to hold a last rep for ten seconds; he felt, psychologically, that it was an important barrier to break through. He stood up and shook his arms out. Then he sat back down on the bench and lifted the weights back up and started another set. This time he pushed himself to a hundred. Again he held the weights out for ten seconds. It felt like his muscles would tear under the strain, but he held it. And he held it. For half a minute he held them there before he let them drop. A hundred reps of forty kilograms. He tried to think of someone else in the gym who he thought could match that, but he couldn't think of one. He had spent over two hours working out already this morning, but he decided to finish off with one more set. This time he reached a hundred and twenty, with another thirty-second hold. He placed the weights back on the rack and strode out and into the locker room. He opened his locker, checked around and took out forty milligrams of Dianabol and swallowed them.

That night, on the doors at the Krazy House, he watched the parade of freaks and geeks stream through. He fucking hated when the agency sent him here but it was the only gig going tonight. It made his skin crawl to look at these people. Girls with shaven heads, lads wearing makeup. Most of them with piercings in their face and fuck knows where else. Skinny boys and chubby girls who looked like something off *The Addams Family*. Some of them, he genuinely couldn't tell if they were male or female. The only upside to working here was that he could take the piss out of them with the other lads on the door, and could arbitrarily refuse entry to anyone that he found particularly odious.

*

Chris and Tommo jumped off the bus on Hannover Street and walked up Wood Street towards the Krazy House, passing the bottle of Smirnoff back and forth. Chris drained the last of it and launched the bottle high in the air and they both sprinted away, hearing the bottle smash behind them on the pavement outside Bar Ca Va a few seconds later. By the time the bouncers came out, they'd be too far away to get the blame for it.

*

Scott stepped outside to check how big the queue was. It was about a hundred yards back, as it usually was at this time. It was half-ten. Most clubs didn't get too busy until after the pubs kicked out but the Krazy House was different. Half the freaks who came here had no chance of getting served in a pub but the Krazy House had a much more relaxed attitude towards checking ID. The unofficial policy was, as long as they weren't too pissed by the time they got there, and if they only looked a bit under eighteen, then let them in. He turned away from the queue and looked down the other way just in time to see a little skate-punk fucker throwing a bottle in the air outside Bar Ca Va. Him and his mate legged it towards him while it smashed behind them. No prizes where they were heading. He felt a first refusal of the night coming on. As they neared, Scott was about to tell them to keep walking, when the one who threw the bottle looked up at him. Scott said nothing. He watched them walk to the back of the queue. He tried to go back inside but his feet were rooted to the spot. He stared at the bottle-thrower. He watched as he got closer and closer as the queue went down. Him and his mate drew level with him and Scott realised the lad was staring back at him. Little fucker. Who did he think he was staring at? Scott watched him walk through the doors. He followed him inside and was about to tell him he wasn't getting in but he couldn't get the words out. He felt a tightening in his chest as he watched the little poof pay his entry fee and start up the metal steps. Before he had time to think, Scott was following him up the steps. He walked a few paces behind him as he and his mate headed straight to the bar. He stood within touching distance of him as they ordered their drinks. He felt the urge to grab his hair and smash his fucking face into the bar, or to take the bottle from his hand and slam it into his face. He felt the tightness in his chest increase, and spreading into his stomach. Some fucking dirgey rock song came on and the two of them turned to run to the dance floor and practically ran into him. The one who threw the bottle stopped while his mate hit the dance floor. He stared up at Scott. Scott clenched his fists and froze on the spot. The fucking little queer smiled at him. *He fucking smiled at him.* Then he carried on to the dance floor. Scott watched him and his mate jumping around like fucking idiots. He took a deep breath and felt the tension in his chest relax a little, and headed back downstairs.

After Scott and the boys clocked off, they usually went straight round to the TwentyFourSeven café round the corner. Scott leaned back in his chair and stretched the tiredness out of his limbs. He let his hands rest on his abdomen. He felt the muscles there through his shirt. He had neglected his abs the last few days. Still very firm, but more work was needed; a set of five hundred sit-ups, the same number of crunches and three hundred launches when he got home would be a good start.

"Fucking hell, look at the state of these, lads."

Marty was looking past Scott. Scott turned his head to look over his shoulder and he saw what his mates were talking about. Two men, obviously fucking queer, were standing at the counter ordering take-out drinks. Marty, Kev and Phil laughed amongst themselves at the sight of them. Scott clenched his fists and shoved them into his pockets. He looked back over his shoulder at the two queers. He clenched his fists so hard he could feel his fingernails cutting into his palms. He stood up and walked past the queers to the toilet and locked himself in. He stared at his reflection in the mirror. He splashed his face with water. He got a flash of the lad he had followed in the Krazy House, then one of the faggot in the pub the other night. He shut his eyes tight and tried to force them out. He opened his eyes and punched his reflection as hard as he could. The mirror cracked. He got control of his breathing and went back to his mates. As he sat down, they were all still watching the two queers.

"Oh, now that's too fucking much," Kev said.

Scott again turned round and saw what had disgusted Kev so much. One of them had rested his head on the other's shoulder and slipped a hand into his back pocket.

"Fucking disgusting," one of the lads said, Scott wasn't sure who.

They paid for their drinks and turned to leave the café. As they approached Scott's table, one of them looked over and registered that he and his boyfriend were being watched. His eyes fleetingly met Scott's but, sensing the aggressive disapproval, quickly looked down. He opened the door and let his boyfriend leave first, and quickly glanced back to see that Scott and the lads were still watching him. The second the door was shut, Scott was on his feet. Without hesitation he followed them out the door and, sensing his purpose, his friends followed him. Scott looked left and right as he got outside the café, and saw the gay boys turning the corner into the alleyway that led to the main road. He didn't run but walked very quickly to catch them up. None of his mates said a word as they followed behind Scott. When they were about twenty yards away, one of the queers turned round to see they were being followed. He grabbed his boyfriend's arm and tried to hurry him up but, not realising what was happening, his boyfriend playfully pulled him back, just as Scott caught up to them. Scott grabbed the back of their necks, one in each hand, and shoved them against the wall.

"Please, just leave us alone, we're not doing any—"

Scott silenced him with a punch to the face.

"Leave him alone," his boyfriend shouted.

"What did you say to me, faggot?"

"Look, we're sorry, just let us go, please."

"Why?" Scott asked. "So you can go home and suck each other's dicks? You fucking dirty pair of shit-stabbers."

Now he started to cry.

"Please," he sobbed, "please, we're not doing anything to you, just leave us alone."

Scott unclenched his fist a little. He lowered his hand to his side as he looked at the look of fear on their faces. Then he got another flash of the Krazy House teen, and punched the sobbing queer in the face. He grabbed his hair and pulled his head down to meet his rising knee. He felt face cartilage smash against his knee, lowered it and brought it straight back up again. Now Kev and the others joined in, Kev smashing the other lad's head against the wall, grinding his face hard into the brickwork. Scott felt the lad go limp in his grip, and let him drop to the floor with a thud. He kicked him hard in the face and heard what was probably his jaw breaking. He looked at his mates taking turns in punching and kicking the other one. Another flash of the boy. He closed his eyes and tried to shake it out. Another flash of *the boy*. He pushed his way through his mates and grabbed hold of the other queer and punched him in the face. He got a flash of the queer from the pub and punched him again. He slammed the back of his head against the wall, and grabbed his shirt to stop him dropping to the ground. He kneed him in the balls. Hard.

"Come 'ead Scott, that'll do, mate," Marty said.

He punched him in the face again.

"Scott, come on, mate, they've had enough," Kev said.

Scott screamed as he punched him in the face, again and again.

"Scott, come on. You'll fucking kill him."

He didn't even know who was talking now, he just kept punching.

"Scott, for fuck's sake, a police car's just gone past."

68

Again and again he punched.

"Come 'ead, lads, let's get out of here."

Scott's friends ran out of the alleyway and Scott let the queer drop to the floor next to his boyfriend. They made awful gurgling sounds as they lay next to each other. Scott looked down and realised he had a hard-on. He kicked them once more each and ran. He ran out of the alleyway and round the corner, past the TwentyFourSeven. He ran back to his car and sped out of town, running red lights and speeding the whole way until he was home. He ran up the stairs and into his bathroom. He stripped off, turned the shower on full blast and got in. Still rock-hard, he took his cock in his hand and began masturbating. He thought of the beating he'd just dished out. He thought of the fear on their faces. He thought of *the boy.* He thought of the cracking of bone and the sight of their blood. He wanked himself hard and thought about the boy. Again and again he thought of the boy. He started to scream as flash after flash of *the boy* assailed his mind, and he was still screaming as he came.

THIRTEEN

Chris pulled the plug out and let the water drain away. He wrapped a towel round his waist and walked onto the landing. He nearly bumped straight into his dad. His dad looked at him.

"Put some bloody clothes on, will you? You're too old to be walking round the house half naked."

It was more than they had said to each other in the last few days. Chris knew why. The way he was feeling, what he was becoming, his dad had seen it in him a long time ago. They had always been close when Chris was little, but things had changed in the last few years. There was a tension between them. They could barely be in the same room at times, and now Chris understood why. His dad knew he was queer and he was ashamed of him.

"Dinner," his mum shouted up the stairs. Chris pulled on his jeans and Ramones T-shirt. He did his fringe with the straighteners he had borrowed from his mum. A bit of eyeliner, also liberated from Mum's makeup bag. He walked down the stairs and into the kitchen. They were both sitting at the table, their dinners half eaten on the table in front of them. Without saying anything, Chris sat down next to his mum. He saw his dad raise half an eye away from his plate, and he *felt* him notice the eyeliner. He felt the disapproval without even seeing his dad shaking his head slightly. Chris pushed the food around his plate disinterestedly.

"You were called five minutes ago. Your dinner's probably gone cold," his dad said. Chris shrugged his shoulders.

"I was getting ready."

"I can see that."

"What's that supposed to mean?"

"Who do you think you're talking to?"

"Who does it look like?"

Billy slammed his cutlery down.

"That's enough," Emily said. "Can we just try to have one meal that doesn't end up in an argument, please?"

"I'm not being spoken to like that in my own fucking house, Emily."

"Billy, there's no need for that language."

"Never mind my fucking language, what about him?"

"What about me?"

"What do you mean, what about me? Look at the fucking state of you, with your skinny fucking T-shirts and your fucking makeup on. You look like a – "

"Like a what, Dad?"

He sat back down.

"Nothing."

"No, go on. Like a what? Like a faggot?"

"Well, you said it, son."

"Yeah, but you were fucking thinking it, weren't you?"

Billy picked up his fork and stabbed it into a potato.

"Weren't you?"

Billy put the potato into his mouth, but his jaw didn't move to chew it. Chris stood up.

"I said, weren't you?"

"Chris, please," Emily said, trying to gently pull him back down by his hand. "Sit down, love."

"I'm not sitting down until he fucking acknowledges me."

Billy chewed slowly and angrily but wouldn't lift his eyes to meet his son's.

"Just answer him, Bill, please."

Still he said nothing, but both Emily and Chris noticed there were tears welling in his eyes. Chris and Emily waited for him to say something but he didn't. Chris swept his own plate and cutlery onto the floor, where it smashed and clattered.

"I'm going out," he said as he left the room.

Chris took the bus into town. He sat alone on the top

deck and swigged angrily from a can of lager. As always, he jumped off the bus on Hannover Street and walked up Wood Street towards the Krazy House. He paid the entry fee and headed straight to the bar on the first floor. He ordered a double vodka and a beer. He slammed the vodka back and sipped his beer as he scoped out the dance floor for familiar faces. It was Thursday night, not the biggest night of the week, but he was hoping that, even though he hadn't arranged to meet anyone, he'd see Tommo or some of the others. There was hardly anyone on the first floor so he took the stairs up to the second floor, killing his beer as he did so. Reaching the second floor, he threw his empty bottle on the floor and ordered another, and another double vodka. He walked to the edge of the dance floor, where a few studenty types were dancing to the Kaiser Chiefs. He watched them, sipping from his beer and necking the vodka, knowing full well just how cool and sexy he must look with the strobes and lights bouncing off him. He noticed a couple of the student girls checking him out. He smiled at them as he poured the beer down his throat. He took the last set of stairs up to the third floor. Still he saw none of his friends, only a few people he was barely on speaking terms with.

Chris thought about talking to Tommo and maybe some of the others, about telling them how he was feeling, and wondered what their reactions might be. Nobody in their circle was gay, not that he knew of, anyway, but it's not like any of them were homophobes or anything like that. They used words like "faggot" at each other sometimes but they didn't even really use it in that way. It was just something to say to each other to take the piss. On balance, he thought they most likely wouldn't really give much of a shit if Chris told them he was gay. Or bi, or whatever he was – he wasn't a hundred percent sure yet. But there was another reason he hadn't said anything to them yet, beyond just worrying about their reactions. Chris liked the secrecy. It was almost like leading a double life, and he wasn't sure he wanted to lose that. Not yet, anyway.

He ordered another beer and double vodka and

72

knocked the spirits back just as he felt his first few kicking in. He noticed someone waving to him on the other side of the dance floor. It took him a few seconds before he realised who it was. He wasn't sure of his name; possibly Carl, but he was someone he'd bought tablets off a few times. And right now, getting fucked up on E, whether his mates were here or not, felt like a very good idea. He crossed the dance floor to Carl and asked if he was carrying anything. In discreet and practised fashion, a gesture heavily disguised as a handshake saw Carl end up twenty quid richer and saw Chris in possession of a bag of five tablets. He didn't even try to look discreet as he threw two of them in his mouth and swallowed them with the last of his beer. He bought another beer and went back down to the second floor. The student girls were still there, dancing to a Strokes song. Chris wasn't a big fan but he felt the need to dance, knowing it would help him come up quicker. The two girls noticed him and covered their mouths with their hands as they spoke into each other's ear. They moved closer to Chris, trying to look all coy as they caught his eye. Chris felt the first wave surging up inside him. Without hesitation, he took another tablet, knowing it was best to capitalise early on the first waves of euphoria. He breathed deep as he felt his every nerve tingling. He eyes rolled back in his head as he felt himself coming up. He stopped dancing and leaned back against a pillar. The girls were now dancing right in front of him. He reached out, feeling the need to have bodily contact with another human being, girl or boy, man or woman. He let his hand rest on the hip of the girl closest to him. He reached his other hand out to the other girl and held the back of her head, her hair feeling so soft. He ran his fingers through it, grateful for the contact. But his mind turned to a different kind of contact. He needed the kind of contact that he had been thinking about for so long, that he had yet to allow himself. He let his hands drop from the girls and walked from the dance floor, much to the girls' confusion, straight down the stairs and out of the club.

    The cold air outside made his skin feel electric, like his flesh was covered in popping candy. He headed down

Wood Street and across Hannover Street, onto Church Street, heading towards the city's gay quarter. Although he had been around this part of town plenty of times in the day, at night, under the influence of vodka and three tabs of ecstasy, it looked and felt completely different. Dance music blared out from every doorway. He felt like he'd been given access to a whole new kingdom. He wandered, dazed, along Whitechapel and Stanley Street. He picked one place at random: Superstar Boudoir. He paid the entry fee and walked in, and was instantly disappointed with what he saw: skinny pretty-boys with vest tops and tight trousers, all gyrating effeminately with each other. This is not what he wanted. He left the Krazy House looking for men and what he found was a bunch of boys that made him look macho. He turned and left and trawled the streets again, looking for something more like what he was looking for. He peeked through the window of club after club, seeing only more of the same; pretty-boys. Where were all the fucking men? Eventually he turned down another street, or what was more like an alleyway. At the bottom right corner, a neon sign that looked like it had been there since the fifties, said simply *The Curzon*. He didn't even need to check inside, not that he could have, with there being no windows, but he instantly knew he was going to find what he wanted in here. He took the last of his two tablets and entered.

He saw right away that he was right. The place was full of real men, along with a few old queens here and there, a few leather-clad clichés. There were screens dotted around the place all playing gay porn. He walked to the bar and ordered himself a drink.

"I'll get that," a satisfyingly masculine voice said. Chris turned to see a man of about forty standing over him.

"Thanks," he said.

"My pleasure. So what's your name?"

"Does it matter?"

The man smiled.

"I suppose it doesn't."

Chris then did the boldest thing of his young life. He

stepped forward and put his hand on the muscular body of the man and kissed him. He felt the rough, stubbly face against his own, such a satisfying contrast to the soft, delicate feel of the girls he'd been with. He felt his cock go instantly rock-hard. The man led him to a booth where they sat and kissed some more. Chris let his hand slide up the man's thigh and onto his cock. It felt huge to him, and as hard as his. After a few more minutes of intense kissing, the man took Chris by the hand and led him downstairs to the toilets. He dragged him into a cubicle and shut the door. Chris felt another wave of euphoria surge through him. He dropped to his knees and took his time sliding the zip of the man's jeans down and opening them to let his cock free. He allowed himself a moment of just staring at it, he wanted to savour this moment for just a few seconds. Then he took it in his mouth and sucked.

FOURTEEN

Lisa unlocked the storage facility. Nick had no idea that she knew about this place, but she had known for a year. She had had to go through one of his competitors, who she had hired to follow him around for a few weeks when his behaviour had become particularly erratic. In truth, there was very little of any real interest uncovered. It was mainly back and forth to various addresses that meant nothing to her, but could easily have been various clients. The only thing that had really intrigued her was this place. A further month of having Nick tailed was enough to establish that there was a pattern to his visits here. He seemed to come here at the start and the end of the week. Lisa had spent the last six months trying to get Nick's keys away from him for long enough to be able to get a copy made of the lock-up key. That had proved extremely difficult, given Nick's paranoia and meticulous nature.

In the end, she had simply swapped the lock-up key for an almost identical looking one immediately after she knew he had made his early week visit, knowing she would be safe for at least a couple of days, in which time she had had a copy made and replaced the decoy key with the original one with Nick being none the wiser. That was a week ago, and yesterday Nick had made his early week visit, so Lisa knew she would be able to take her time here today.

The clanging metal sound of the door sliding open jolted her and made her heart beat faster. She felt along the wall for a light-switch and as she found it she closed her eyes and flicked the light on. She didn't have a clue what to expect when she opened her eyes, but she prepared herself for something shocking. She was almost disappointed when she opened her eyes to reveal nothing but a safe and a table and chair. She walked over to the table and saw a photo album on it. She flicked through it, finding only pictures of what she assumed was Nick, aged about twelve, with his mother. The mother that had killed herself when he was thirteen. The mother who he refused to talk about. The mother that had checked out on him and left him to be raised by a monster.

She walked over to the safe and examined it. She took out her iPhone and typed the name and make of the safe into Google and found a page with extensive info on it. She sat at the table and spent a few minutes reading up on it. A six-number pass code. She walked to the safe and entered 260809 – Monica's birthday. The bleep and the red light on the safe told her that was wrong. Next she tried 130602 – their wedding date. Wrong again. She tried her own date of birth, and Nick's. Both wrong. She was relieved to find that this safe didn't lock you out after three failed attempts as she'd anticipated, and wracked her brains. She tried to think like her husband for a minute, and then it hit her. 080389 – Nick's thirteenth birthday. A date significant not because it was a birthday but for one huge reason. It was the day Nick's mum took her own life, therefore probably the most significant day in his life. She punched it in and this time she got a green light and the clunk of the bolts sliding open. She took a deep breath and opened the safe. She gasped aloud as she saw the huge pile of money in there. She picked a stack of the cash up and flicked through it. It wasn't kept in any kind of order. Fives were lumped in with tens, twenties and fifties. There had to be thousands there. Tens of thousands, easily. She reached into the bottom of the safe and lifted out the item wrapped in an oily old rag. From the heft and shape, she already knew what it must be as she unwrapped it, but when she opened it to confirm it was indeed a gun, she almost vomited. She had never even been near one before. She wondered what Nick could possibly need a gun for, and how she could have stayed married for so long to a man she now realised she barely knew.

FIFTEEN

Scott followed the boy up the stairs and onto the dance floor. The dance floor was empty except for the two of them. Smoke surrounded them. Scott felt eyes on him from inside the smoke, but he could see nobody else. The boy danced in front of him, his eyes locked on Scott's. Scott clenched his eyes closed; when he opened them the boy was gone. He looked down to see him on his knees, Scott's cock in his mouth. Scott screamed but no sound came out. The boy looked up at him, still sucking. Scott heard a soft voice say his name from somewhere in the smoke.

"Who's there?"

"Me, Scott."

He turned to his right to see Carrie standing there, naked. He tried to look at her as his cock was sucked, but his eyes were dragged back to the boy. He pulled his cock out of his mouth and asked Carrie to do what he had done, but she refused. He turned back to the boy, flipped him over and began fucking him hard, his eyes moving back and forth between him and Carrie as he did.

Scott woke up, and took a second to realise he was in his own bed. The sheets were soaked through with sweat and his cock was hard. This was the third night in a row that he'd dreamt about *the boy*, the dreams becoming increasingly vivid. He could control his thoughts to some extent, he could block certain thoughts out. But in his dreams there was no escape from them. There was no hiding place from these images. He imagined drilling a hole into his head, to let those thoughts out. He'd read about them doing it with people who were mad or possessed, hundreds of years ago. He wondered if there was some way for him to do it. Or if there was a modern equivalent to it. He wondered if it was possible that someone had planted these thoughts in there to mess with his head for some reason, but realised how paranoid that sounded. He thought it must be the steroids. He'd have to change them. Yeah, the steroids, that's probably what all this shit was about. He wasn't like that, he wasn't turning queer. He just needed to change his steroids again.

He got out of bed and did a thousand stomach crunches, followed by three hundred push-ups. He did them effortlessly. He grabbed his free weights and did two hundred and fifty each of shoulder lifts and arm reps. He did these in front of the window, wearing only his boxer shorts. The bunch of schoolgirls at the bus stop opposite his flat would have a clear view of him if they looked up, and he was happy about that. He looked at them, made himself focus on their legs in their shorts skirts and knee-high socks. No red-blooded male would see them and not wanna fuck them. If he could compartmentalise the thoughts about boys and men, limit them only to in his sleep, and bombard his own mind with thoughts and images of women and girls, if he could keep the two separate, it wouldn't be so bad. He had to find a way to keep them separate.

He showered and picked out some smart-looking clothes. He was meeting Carrie in an hour, and he wanted to be looking his best. Last week's meeting with her had gone pretty well, he'd thought. Better than he was anticipating. It was important than he made another good impression today. It was just coffee again, no big talks on the agenda, just a coffee and a chat. Like a date really.

He got to the Starbucks early and ordered them both a drink. He kept his eyes on the door, waiting for her to arrive. When she did, he was pleased to see that she had also dressed to impress. This gave him some renewed positivity: if she was trying to look good for him, she must be thinking seriously about them getting back together. Of course, it was also possible that she was now dressing to impress *other* men. For a second, his head was filled with an image of her fucking another man. He pushed the image away and stood to greet her.

"Hiya, babes," he said, leaning in to peck her on the cheek.

"Hiya, Scott," she said, accepting the kiss, but not reciprocating.

"How've you been?"

"OK. You?"

"Yeah, I'm fine, Carrie. Better for seeing you, obviously. I'm really glad you came."

She turned and looked out of the window. She bit her bottom lip and looked like she was trying to control herself, to stop herself from crying.

"What is it?"

"I've been thinking about us a lot since I last saw you."

Scott's face dropped, along with his heart. His grip tightened around his huge coffee mug, so much so that it felt like it was about to shatter.

"What have you been thinking?"

"Lots of things. I've been missing you. I've been thinking how we're much better together than we are apart."

His grip loosened on his mug, just as it was about to break.

"But things can't be like they were before," Carrie continued, the tears filling up her eyes now. "If we get back together... things have to change."

"They will, Carrie. I mean it, I'm a changed man. I've stopped the steroids already, just like you asked."

"There's more to it than that, though, there have to be more changes."

"Just name them. Whatever you want."

"OK," she said, trying to wipe the tears out of her eyes without smudging her makeup, "well, for starters, I want us to go to couples counselling. To Relate, or something like that."

"Come on, Carrie, we don't need counselling – "

"I mean it, Scott. This is a deal breaker. If you want us back together, then this is something I want you to do. Something I need you to do."

Scott looked down at his hands, suddenly self-conscious and unsure of what to do with them. He lay them flat on the table.

"Alright. I'll do it. We'll go to couples counselling."

She put one of her hands on top of his. He turned his hand over and held hers.

"Good. And there's one more thing."

"What?"

"I want you to do something about your anger levels. I know you've stopped the steroids, and that's great, but you had problems with anger management before you even started on them. You've scared me sometimes, Scott, even before you... before what happened."

"Really? I scare you?"

"You have done, yeah. Sometimes."

He let go of her hand and sat back in his chair.

"Fucking hell. I had no idea. I'm so ashamed of that. I'm so sorry."

She reached across and took his hand again. This time he felt like *he* might cry.

"It's alright. I know you never meant to."

"So what do you want me to do?"

"I don't know, there's lots of things you can do. I know you don't like the idea of counselling, but there's other things you can try. Like meditation."

He couldn't help but burst out laughing. Carrie joined in, and the feeling of relief, the feeling of them sharing something like a laugh, almost overwhelmed him.

"Meditation? Can you really see me sitting in a room full of hippies and old woman going 'ommmmmmm'?"

Carrie laughed harder.

"It's not like that. I've been trying it myself lately."

"What, seriously?"

"Yeah. I go to a class at the community centre on Thursday nights. And it's not like you'd think, it's just normal people there. A lot of blokes, too."

"Fucking hell, the thought of me going to a meditation class," he said, shaking his head. "But OK. I'll give it a go.

For you."

He squeezed her hand and smiled.

"To the centre of the city, where all roads meet."

PART TWO: IMPASSES

SIXTEEN

Nick took a swig from his hip flask. Surveillance work. He hated it. But he knew the surveillance aspect of this job was the easy part. It was about to get much uglier. He adjusted his wing mirror so he could see the front gate of the house. His rear-view was giving him a reasonable view of the front door of the house, but it wasn't good enough. They had been inside for about half an hour so he decided it was safe for him to get a closer look.

He got out of the car and closed the door, checking the street in both directions. He crouched down as he silently opened the front gate and passed through it. The front curtains were closed but there was a tiny gap between them. With the cover of the semi-darkness of early evening, Nick felt bold enough to put his face right up to the glass, tilting his head for a better view. Squinting, he could make out part of a couch on the other side of the room. And on it, he could make out parts of two naked bodies. One male, one female. The woman was on top of the man. He couldn't make out faces but he already knew who it was. This was the house of Derek Lynch, one of his clients. Lynch had a contract with HTSS; Nick had updated his security system for him just last month, but tonight's job was off the books. Nick went back to his car and waited.

An hour later he saw a man, mid-twenties, good-looking in a catalogue model kind of way, open the front door, take a cursory look around and leave the house. Nick slipped quietly out of his car and caught up to him just as he was about to put his car key in the door. Nick grabbed a fistful of hair and slammed his face into the roof of his car. Catalogue boy went down like a sack of shit. Nick grabbed him by the collar and dragged him down an alleyway at the side of

Lynch's house, throwing him to the floor between two wheelie bins.

"Take the money, just take it," he said, pulling his wallet out of his arse pocket and holding it up to Nick. Nick kicked it out of his hand and punched him square in the face. His nose instantly exploded, covering the bottom half of his face in blood.

"I'm not interested in your fucking money," Nick said, kicking him in the abdomen. He felt a couple of ribs crack.

"Wh... wh... what then?" he managed to gasp out as he sucked air in.

Nick crouched down and slapped him back and forth across the face a few times.

"Your name is David Moore. You live at 28 Alwyn Street and you work at the Next in Liverpool One."

"What... how do you know?" David asked.

"Your mum and dad live at 17 Leicester Street, your sister Jackie lives there too, when she's not at uni in Manchester."

"Who are you?"

"Who I am isn't important. What's important is who the woman you've just been fucking is. Or more to the point, who her husband is. You do know who Derek Lynch is, don't you?"

David nodded his head meekly. Nick punched him in the kidneys.

"Speak the fuck up, David."

"Yes. Yes, I know who he is."

"Good. Then you'll presumably also know that he's a man of wealth and influence. And, if you didn't already, then I hope you are now understanding that Derek isn't gonna tolerate you sticking your dick in his wife's cunt. Or any of her holes, for that matter. I know, David, you were just thinking you'd found yourself a rich milf to fuck, maybe to spend a bit of cash on you. But you've picked the wrong milf in this instance. Now, you're a good-looking lad, if slightly less so now. I'm sure you can have your pick of desperate housewives. But you will not contact Mrs Lynch again. Ever."

Nick stood back up.

"Give me your phone," he said.

"Why? I thought you weren't interested in—"

Nick shut him up with another kick to the guts. Nick thought he heard David losing control of his bladder, the smell that hit his nostrils a few seconds later confirming it.

"Just fucking give it to me."

David reached into his pocket and pulled out his mobile. Nick threw it on the floor and stamped on it a few times.

"Now, I'm hoping you haven't memorised her number. If you have, then I urge you to forget it right now."

Nick knelt back down, the smell of piss causing him to lean back a bit.

"Do we understand each other, David?"

David, nodded, managing a strangled "yes" through the tears. Nick reached into his pocket and pulled out a roll of pound coins. He clenched it tightly in his fist.

"Now, David, I know you've taken a pasting, but this one is from Derek."

Nick lifted David, now resigned and compliant, into a more upright sitting position. He put his fist right in front of David's nose and slowly drew it back.

"Please, no more," David sobbed.

"Shut up."

"Please, please don't hurt me anymore."

"I said shut the fuck up."

Nick could hardly understand what David was saying now, he was just spouting incomprehensible shit through the sobbing.

"Don't hurt me anymore," he managed to say. "Please, I'm sorry."

"Fucking shut up! You fucking cry baby. You fucking stupid nancy boy. Be a fucking man."

Nick punched him full in the face, stopping the crying.

"Now, take a minute, then get yourself home. And if

you come near her again, I'll break both your fucking legs, then I'll pay your family a little visit."

Nick went back to his car and took some long, slow, deep breaths until he felt his heart rate slowing down. He swigged thirstily from his hip flask before driving away, the smell of piss still stinging his nostrils.

*

Absolutely pathetic. The same routine. Every fucking time. Nick sat in his car outside Cedar Nursing Home. Hunched over the steering wheel, his knuckles turning white as he gripped it. His hip flask drained dry, and the bile rising up from his guts. All the familiar things that happened every time he came here. He took a deep breath and forced himself out of the car, grabbing the box of pastries and the two coffees that he'd picked up from the nearby deli on the way. He entered and braced himself for the smell of more piss and shit as he passed through the main lounge. He stopped by the staff room, urging them all to help themselves to a Danish or a pain au chocolat. He carried the few remaining ones through to his dad's room.

"Alright, Dad?"

"Oh, look who it is, seed of my fucking loins."

Nick put the pastries and one of the coffees down in front of his dad.

"Bought you some pastries, Dad."

"So I see. Suppose you've been showing off by sharing them all out with the staff, have you?"

"I gave a few of the staff some, yeah."

"Make you feel good about yourself, did it?"

"No, I was just – "

"Just being a 'good guy'. Oh, they all love you here. They all think you're such a good guy. Such a nice bloke. You've got them all fooled, haven't you, Nick?"

"I don't know what you mean, Dad."

"Yes, you fucking do, you little nancy boy. Coming here glad-handing, doling out your poncey fucking pastries" – he swept the box onto the floor – "acting the fucking part. The dutiful son who pays for the best care for his father, who visits regularly, who's nice and friendly to the staff. None of them know what you're really like, do they, Nick? But I do. Your old dad knows, doesn't he?"

"So you're telling me you don't like the pastries, then?"

"Don't try and be fucking clever with me, boy. And clear that fucking mess up."

"I'm not fucking clearing it up." Nick forced out a laugh, his hands already starting to shake. "You knocked them on the floor, you clear them up."

"You fucking what?"

"You heard me, Dad." This time his voice shook too. "You get them."

"You think you're too fucking big for a good hiding, boy? 'Cause, believe me, you're not. Now fucking get that shit picked up."

Nick hesitated, then did what they both knew he was going to do. He gave in. He put down his coffee and tidied up the mess his father had made, then he took his usual place sitting on the edge of the bed. John began nibbling at a croissant.

"There. That's better. Now, why haven't you brought my granddaughter with you?"

"She's in school, Dad."

"Not just today, you stupid fuck." John threw the croissant at Nick. It hit him on the side of the head and dropped to the floor. Nick picked it up. "I mean in general. I haven't seen her for months now. It's not right, keeping a man from seeing his grandchild. It's not right by me and it's not right by her."

"I'm not keeping her from seeing you." Nick began fiddling with the croissant, realised what he was doing and put it back down. "We've just been a bit busy, that's all."

"You should never be too busy to do something like that. You just make sure you bring her soon."

"Yeah, of course I will."

Nick envisaged another argument where he tried to persuade Lisa that they had to let Monica see her granddad, knowing she wouldn't allow it, and knowing deep down that he didn't want her and his dad spending time together himself.

"Yeah, sure you will. As long as the missus allows it, eh? She says what goes in your house, doesn't she?"

"No. It's not like that at all."

John burst out laughing.

"Yeah, not fucking much, it isn't. She always was a stuck-up little tart, that one."

"Dad, don't... please don't talk about her like that."

"Why not? The truth hurt, does it?"

"No. It's... she's my wife, Dad."

"Yeah, and you're obviously not giving her enough of the good stuff. I bet that's all she needs, a good fucking seeing to. Tell you what, send her over and I'll give her what she needs."

"Dad, for fuck's sake." Nick had meant to shout, but realised he had started crying, and it had come out as a plaintive plea.

"Oh, here we fucking go, here come the waterworks. You fucking pansy. Look at you, blubbing like a fucking girl."

Nick held his head in his hands.

"Please, Dad, don't."

"God, you're fucking pathetic. 'Oh, please, Dad, please, Dad'. What kind of man are you? Letting yourself be bossed around by some tart, crying in front of your father. It's about time you manned up."

"And how do I do that, Dad? Do I beat my wife? Do I beat my child? Like you did? Is that how I be a man?"

"Oi! Now I only ever raised my hand to your mother when she deserved it, and the same with you. Someone needed to toughen you up a bit."

"Oh, well, a great fucking job of that you did."

"Yeah, I can see. Obviously, I didn't do it enough, did I?"

Nick stood up, wiping the tears from his eyes and regaining his composure.

"Look, I'd better get going. I've got lots of work to do."

"Oh, yeah, of course, gotta go and play at being grown up, haven't you? You're the big swinging fucking dick at work, aren't you? Imagine what they'd all say if they could see you now. Alright, fine. Go and do your work. But remember to bring me my granddaughter."

*

Nick pushed open the door of his house to complete silence. He'd expected, and hoped, to hear the sound of Monica laughing and playing. He realised it was nearly nine o'clock, way past her bedtime. He hung his coat up and walked through to the living room. Lisa was sitting on the couch with her back to him. She lifted a glass of white wine to her lips and took a big swig. Nick clocked the half-empty bottle on the table beside her. He did a quick calculation; assuming she'd put Monica to bed at about half-seven, that probably meant this was her first bottle.

"Evening," he said.

Lisa turned her head half to the side.

"That's all you've got to say?"

"Well... yeah. What else do you expect me to say?"

"What day is it?"

"What?"

"Today. What day is it?"

"It's Tuesday evening, Lisa. Where are you going with this?"

"And what day were you last here?"

"What day?"

"Yes Nick, what day?"

Nick scratched his head and tried to cast his mind back.

"Saturday?"

"Yes. Saturday. You haven't set foot inside your own home for three whole days, Nick. Where have you been?"

"Where do you think I've been? I've been working. I've been busy."

"Don't do that."

"Don't do what?"

"Don't try and fob me off with that stock response.

91

You think as soon as you mention work that you can just shut me down, that I can't possibly be allowed to question you. It's just fobbing me off and I'm sick of it."

"Lisa, you know the score. We agreed a long time ago that some things I do... when it comes to work... it's just best that you don't know. Some things you wouldn't want to know. And I sure as shit don't want you to know. I need to keep things compartmentalised. I need to do what I need to do for work, then when I come through that door, I need to leave it behind."

"But that's just it, Nick. You don't leave it behind. You carry it with you, the things you do. It all hangs over you. There's a fucking huge cloud following you around. You're out of the house at all hours, for days on end. Sometimes you come home and you have blood on you, for fuck's sake."

"Lisa, this is what I'm talking about. This is contrary to the agreement we made years ago. An agreement that said you would not ask me about the things I do. You understood that I would have to do things that are ugly, things that are... different to what most people do to earn a living. I made it clear that what I do can earn us a lot of money. Many times more than what I could have ever hoped to earn if I'd stayed in the police. I made it clear that you would enjoy the benefits of that. That you'd never want for anything. That I would provide for you and Monica. But the pay-off for that is that you don't do exactly what you're doing now. That you wouldn't fucking cross-examine me like this. This is not what you agreed with me, Lisa."

"I know it's not, but I can't do it anymore. I can't stick to this don't-ask-don't-tell policy we've had. Not anymore. Because you've broken your part of the agreement too."

"What the fuck do you mean? I've kept my side of it. Look at this fucking house, look at the fucking clothes you wear, the car you drive, the school Monica goes to. How the fuck have I not kept my side of the agreement?"

"Because you no longer keep the two sides separate. In fact I'm not sure you ever did. You're slipping, Nick.

You're falling apart. And I know you're back on the drugs, and I know you're drinking. You're spending longer and longer away from home. You're drinking and doing fuck knows what drugs. You're so fucking secretive. I don't know what's going on inside your head, but I know it's bad. And controlling you, like some fucking puppet master, is Michael fucking Epson."

"We owe Michael Epson. We owe him big. If it wasn't for him I wouldn't have half the clients I've got. We wouldn't have what we've got."

"But that doesn't mean he gets to own your fucking soul, Nick. That doesn't mean he gets to own my fucking husband, to own my fucking family. I don't know what it is between the two of you, but I know he has a hold over you, just like your dad does. What is it with you being drawn to these powerful older men?"

"What do you mean?"

"Epson is just some kind of bizarre extension of your relationship with your dad. It's exactly the same dynamic. He says jump, you ask how high. He clicks his fingers and you come running. Every time. I hate this hold those two have over you. I'm fucking sick of it."

"Well I'm fucking sick of this, Lisa. I came home to relax for a few hours, and I come home to this shit."

He turned back towards the front door.

"Don't you walk out on me now, Nick. We need to talk about this."

Nick walked towards the front door.

"Nick, don't you fucking leave."

But he was already out the door. Lisa picked up her empty wine glass and hurled it at the front door, screaming Nick's name. She collapsed to her knees, sobbing.

"Mummy?"

The faint voice from the top of the stairs. Lisa turned to see Monica sitting on the top stair, her teddy in her hand. She walked to her and picked her up and carried her back towards her room, whispering that everything was OK, knowing things hadn't been OK in her home for a long time, and that nothing was going to be OK ever again.

SEVENTEEN

Steven Mitchell, or Mitch to those who knew him well, was a man who had known anger. He had been angry for a large part of his life. Abandoned by his mother, a habitual drug user who had lost custody of Mitch when he was six, he had spent most of his childhood in care. He had been through several sets of foster parents, his difficult behaviour always proving just too much for even the most dedicated of families. He had never known who his father was, and this lack of identity and a decent male role-model only further increased the anger he carried around with him at all times. His teens brought trouble with the police, and several stays in young offender institutions, mainly for car theft and other petty crime. At the age of nineteen he graduated to burglary, and took his first hit of adult prison. It was during his two-year spell in prison that he met Jake Watson. Jake was three-quarters of the way through a fifteen-year sentence for armed robbery. During his spell inside, Jake had discovered Buddhism through an older con who had taken Jake under his wing. Now Jake, in turn, had seen something in Mitch, something that reminded him of himself; a young man, filled with rage and heading in only one direction. Just as had been done to him nearly a decade before, Jake took Mitch under his wing. At first he met resistance and then indifference but he wasn't prepared to give up easily, and his persistence began, little by little, to pay off. Eventually Mitch let his guard down and he and Jake became close. Even when they had become friends, Mitch had retained a strong scepticism around Jake's Buddhism, but seeing the serenity it brought, he became curious about that too. Jake showed him how to meditate, and the first time he tried it, it was like he had come home. He experienced an instant epiphany, and from then on he was changed. He started meditating for at least an hour every day and began studying Buddhist philosophy. Over the next few months, he became a model prisoner. Such was the change in him that he ended up serving only half his sentence.

That was over twenty years ago, and now, every Thursday, he gave up an evening of his time to teach a meditation class to twenty people in his local community centre. Although he was open about his Buddhism, he made no attempt to add a Buddhist slant to the classes, though many of the people who took the class became curious about it and asked him many questions, some joining him at the local Buddhist centre. He took no payment for his time, even paying the nominal fee required to hire the room out of his own pocket.

It was into this room, in this community centre, that Scott Collins now walked. He walked to the back of the room and rolled out Carrie's yoga mat that he had borrowed for this purpose. He noticed a few of the other people doing stretches and warm-ups, and decided to follow suit, just to have something to do with his hands and hide the huge fear and embarrassment he was currently feeling. He looked at the people around him and was quite surprised by how normal most of them looked. He had expected a room full of dreadlocked hippies and New-Agey women. There were a couple of people who looked like they embodied the stereotype but the rest of them just looked like anyone you might pass on the street. And there were several other men there.

"Alright, everybody," the man at the front of the class said, "shall we get started?"

Scott assumed this man was Mitch, who he had spoken to briefly on the phone. Everyone sat down cross-legged on their mats. Scott did likewise.

"Let's start off with some deep breathing. Everybody close your eyes. Now, with your palms facing up on your knees, pinch your thumbs and your fingers together. Breathe in deeply through the nose and slowly out through the mouth."

Scott took a look around the room. Everyone was

doing exactly as instructed. He looked to the front of the room. Mitch was looking right at him. He was gripped by a sudden fear and panic. He considered just standing up and walking straight out of there. Mitch held his gaze for a second, then, very slowly and deliberately, gave him an almost invisible nod of the head. Scott wasn't sure what the gesture meant, what it signified, but something in it made him stay.

He crossed his legs in the same way everyone else had. He closed his eyes and pushed his thumbs and middle fingers together. He tuned in to Mitch's voice.

"Deep breaths in through the nose and out through the mouth. Let all the thoughts in your head dissipate. Whatever thoughts have been filling your head today, whether it's problems at work, stresses at home, whatever it is, just let it all fade away. Focus only on your breathing and only on my voice."

Scott slowed his breathing right down and synched it into rhythm with Mitch's voice. He felt the tension in his shoulders reducing. His head felt as though it had become weightless, like it was hovering above his shoulders. The knot of nervous energy in the pit of his stomach, he hadn't even realised it was there until now, but he suddenly became fully aware of not just its presence but its equally sudden unravelling. Just as quickly as it had made itself known to him, it seeped away, turning into a light, tingly feeling that spread out from his stomach and seemed to dissolve into his bloodstream, flowing to his extremities.

"Let your neck become loose, let your head roll around your shoulders slowly. First clockwise, then anticlockwise."

Scott did as instructed. The feeling inside him spread to his neck as he rolled his head around, clockwise and anticlockwise. Even the backs of his eyeballs seemed infused with this inexplicable feeling that he had never experienced before.

Fifty minutes later, Scott opened his eyes and felt reborn. He felt moved to his core, like something profound had just happened to him. It was like waking up from the best sleep of his life, feeling totally refreshed. He stood up and stretched his limbs out. He watched as a few of the people approached Mitch and shook his hand, telling him they'd see him next week. He folded up his mat deliberately slowly to give everyone else time to say whatever they wanted to say to Mitch then get out so he could speak to him with a bit of privacy. He wasn't sure what he was going to say but he knew he simply had to speak with him. He waited until everyone else had left the room and approached him as he rolled up his own mat.

"Alright, Mitch?"

He turned round and faced him.

"Yeah. I'm guessing you're Scott?"

"That's right, yeah. We spoke on the phone the other day."

"Sure. So how did you find it?"

"Erm, really good, actually. A lot better than I was expecting, to be honest with you."

"Yeah, I noticed you seemed a bit unsure of yourself at the start there."

"I was. Sorry, mate, I didn't mean to seem disrespectful or nothing. It's just... well... to tell you the truth, I've been... erm... I've had a few..."

Scott couldn't finish his sentence; he couldn't even finish the thought. But now, it was suddenly as though a valve he never knew existed had been opened, his hands began to shake and, to his horror, he realised that he had started to cry.

"God, what the fuck is wrong with me?" he managed to say as he dropped down onto one knee. Mitch knelt down beside him and gently placed a hand on his shoulder.

"It's alright, man, just let it out, let all that shit out of you. It's alright."

"Fuck. Fucking hell. What's happening?"

"You'd be surprised how often that happens. You're about the tenth person I've seen this happen to. It's fine. You're fine."

"I'm not fine," Scott said, finally regaining some composure. "I mean, don't get me wrong, that was great, it

98

was really great, but I felt like something clicked inside of me. I know it sounds stupid – "

"It doesn't sound stupid at all. Go on."

"I've had so much... I don't know, I've been having a tough time lately. A few... problems. I don't know how to explain it. I've had lots of... lots of thoughts, and I don't know what to do, what I can..."

"It's OK, Scott. I think I know where you're coming from."

"Really?"

"I think so. Can I speak frankly with you?"

"Yes."

"I could sense it in you from the moment you walked in. You carried it with you."

"What?"

"Your anger, Scott. And standing here now, I can sense it in you. The anger, I know it's there. I know because I found it in myself. A long time ago, a great man reached out to me and helped me get control of my anger. My violence. And I know you carry violence with you, Scott."

"Is it that obvious?"

"Scott, I can practically smell the violence on you."

"Can... can you help me?"

"I can. If you come back here next week, I can give you some books to read, some CDs to listen to, and I think what you can learn in this room can be of help to you, Scott. I really do."

Mitch stood up and reached down towards Scott. Scott took his hand and let him help him to his feet.

"So you think you'll be back next week?"

"Definitely, Mitch. I'll be here alright."

EIGHTEEN

Life is a series of firsts. It is defined by them. Your first day at school. Your first ride of your bike. Your first kiss. Your first drink. These are important landmarks. Right now, the first that was occupying space in Christian McGann's mind was his first cock. He had had it three nights ago, and right now he felt defined by it. It was all he could think about. He lay on his bed, his own hard cock in his hand, replaying the night in The Curzon. The feeling of it in his mouth, the taste of the come. And now, he had to have more.

He rolled off his bed and grabbed his phone, opening the Grindr app he had downloaded. He had set himself up with a profile on the site this morning. He had filled in the basic info – his age, his eye colour, etc. – but he had yet to fill in much detail. Now he filled in what he was looking for. Casual, no-strings sex, preferably with older, muscular men. A bit of rough stuff, a bit of role play. Only decent-looking guys need apply. He leant back and thought for a moment. He remembered how skint he currently was. He wondered how he was going to pay for this weekend's drink and drugs. He clicked on "edit profile" and added one nota bene. Chris added that he would lower his otherwise strict rules about only going with good-looking guys as long as the price was right. It wasn't really prostitution. It was a way to ensure that this weekend's drink and drugs would be paid for and that he got to fuck some more men while he was at it.

*

Michael Epson kissed his wife goodnight. He told her he was heading back into the office for a couple of hours, and that she should not wait up for him. He walked out to the Jag and headed through the electric security gates and out of Formby. He hit the city centre a few minutes later. He drove through the Liverpool night, taking in the sights and sounds of the city he loved. It was only a Wednesday night, but you would have thought it was a Friday or Saturday, such were the hordes of revellers. He drove into the underground parking area of the office building and parked up. He took the stairs up to the lobby. Clive, the old Jamaican guy who manned the reception security desk, nodded in greeting. Epson came here this late frequently, so there was nothing out of the ordinary about this late-night visit. He took the lift up to the top floor and walked through the outer office. He loved being here at night, alone. He loved the gentle hum of the servers mixing with the noises floating up from the street. He went into his office and switched the computer on, singing into Gaydar. He took out his phone and logged into his Grindr account and searched for who was online. He clicked onto a few profiles and was disappointed to find mostly muscle Marys and men that made him look youthful. He changed his search criteria to cut out anyone over the age of twenty-one. The first few he scrolled past didn't have a photo on their profile so he ignored them. Then one thumbnail profile picture caught his eye. *Punkboy.* He clicked on it and enlarged the profile pic. He was gorgeous, and just Michael's type: pretty face, stunning eyes, blond fringe half-covering one of them. His age was listed as eighteen but Michael suspected he might even be a year or two younger than that. At least he hoped so. Michael read his profile. Punkboy was into older men but had quite high standards. Michael's heart sank a bit. He may be many things but he knew he had never been much of a looker. But then, at the bottom of his profile, it stated that, if the price was right, he would lower those exacting standards. Michael typed out a brief and to-the-point message and sent it. He leant back in his chair and waited for a response. He put his iPod in the dock he kept on his desk and selected some Mozart. He turned the sound up, closed his eyes and felt the music flowing through him. He wasn't an expert on music by any means, but he loved classical. It was the least demanding form of music and, he admitted to himself, it was shorthand for the kind of sophistication he wanted to portray. For all his millions, he was still a Bootle boy at heart, and the trappings of wealth he accumulated, the expensive art, the designer clothes, he didn't really understand them. He had an assistant select the art, and his wife selected the clothes. Most people who had come from humble beginnings to attain great wealth were at pains to highlight their working-class origins. Michael was the opposite. While he publicly often spoke of his humble origins and his pride in his working-class roots, in truth it was all PR bullshit. Michael wanted to put as much distance as possible between where he had started and where he had ended up, and he clung to as many of the affectations of wealth as possible to drown out that old image.

The sound of a message pinging in his Grindr inbox interrupted the sound of music. He was pleased to see it was from *Punkboy*. Michael's offer of fifty pounds for a mutual blowjob had been deemed acceptable. He picked up his mobile and called the number programmed into his speed dial.

"Hello?"

"Nick, it's Michael. I have a little errand for you to run."

*

Nick turned onto the main road and stopped at the lights. He gripped the steering wheel and thought about turning left and heading back out of town to home. He wasn't sure how long he could keep doing this for Epson. He did a U-turn by the Tesco and headed back up Aigburth Road and turned left and pulled up outside the address Michael had given him. He looked up at the front-bedroom window and saw the light get switched off. Half a minute later the front door opened and a good-looking kid came out, putting his jacket on as he closed the door behind him. He bent down to the passenger's window and Nick leaned over and opened the door.

"Hi," the kid said as he got in. Nick saw in close-up just how good-looking this boy was. "I'm Chris."

"Nick."

"So where are we going?"

"The Radisson."

"The hotel?"

"That's right," Nick said as he executed a three-point

turn and headed back in the direction of town. "Ever been there before?"

"No."

"Really? Surely you've had a few high-powered business meetings in their conference facilities?"

Chris laughed.

"No, I prefer the facilities at the Echo Arena personally. So, this fella I'm meeting. Got a few quid, has he?"

"Just a few, yeah."

"I should have charged more than fifty," Chris said.

"Fifty? Fucking hell."

Nick turned to look at him.

"Not being funny, Chris, but you could add a zero onto that. Good-looking lad like you? You'd be worth more than fifty quid, mate. That's assuming I approved of you selling yourself at all. Which I don't."

"So why are you picking me up for this fella?"

Nick reached for his cigarettes.

"That's a very good question," he said, offering the box to Chris, who took one and lit it up. Nick opened Chris's window a crack for him to blow the smoke out.

"And the answer?"

"Is complicated."

"Isn't everything? So what are you, his driver?"

"No. I'm... a lot of things to this man."

"Like what?"

"Well, my official title would be 'security consultant'. That's what it says on my business card anyway."

"What the fuck does a security consultant do?"

Nick blew a cloud of smoke out of his window.

"Again, good question. To be honest, I'm still trying to figure that one out myself."

Chris laughed again. He leaned forward and opened the glove box and flicked through some of the CDs in there.

"Wow, you're into The Clash?"

"Amongst other things."

"Beastie Boys, New Order; some good stuff in here.

You've got good taste. For an old man."

"Cheeky bastard."

"Oh, fucking hell. Coldplay? I take it all back."

"That's not mine. That's the missus'."

"Oh, yeah, of course it is."

"It fucking is. Here, watch."

Nick swiped the CD from Chris's hand and Frisbee'd it out of the window onto the Dock Road.

"There, that's how much I think of fucking Coldplay."

They both laughed.

"Anyway, we're here now."

Nick pulled into the car park of the Radisson and parked. They both got out and Chris followed Nick towards the front door. The doorman nodded to Nick.

"Evening, Mr Hanman."

"Evening, Paul," Nick replied.

They walked into the busy lobby. Nick stopped and put his hand on Chris's shoulder, turning him in the direction he was pointing.

"See those lifts?"

Chris nodded.

"Up to the fifth floor. Room five-two-three."

He turned him to his right.

"See that bar?"

Chris nodded again.

"That's where I'll be. Alright?"

Chris headed towards the lift. Nick watched him go. As he pressed the button for the lift, he turned back to Nick. Christ, he looked young. Like a child. Nick nodded to him as the lift doors opened, then walked into the bar and took a seat on a barstool.

"Yes, sir?"

"Pint of Staropramen, please, mate."

The barman pulled the pint and placed it down.

"A shot of Jim Beam too, please."

Nick knocked the shot back and drained about half the pint. He stared deep into the glass. He leaned back in his chair and looked out of the bar into the lobby. From where he was, he could just about see the lifts. He looked back at his drink. He took another swig of it and jumped down off the stool. He marched to the lift and pressed the call button. He looked up at the arrow and saw it was on the third floor and heading up. He turned towards the other lift just as its doors closed. He burst through the door to the staircase and bounded up them three at a time. He walked out onto the fifth floor, gasping for breath. He didn't need to check the room numbers, he'd been to this room plenty of times before. He stopped outside room 523. He clenched his fist and was about to knock on the door, but stopped. He turned away from the door. Then he turned back and lifted his hand again. This time he didn't even get it close to the door. He trudged slowly back to the lift and headed back down to the bar.

Two and a half pints later, Nick felt a tap on his shoulder. He turned round to see Chris. His hair was damp from the shower he had presumably just taken. It made him look even younger now than he did before, and Nick wished he had knocked on the door.

"Alright?"

Chris nodded his head slightly.

"Drink?"

"Yeah, please."

Nick signalled for the barman.

"Another two of these, please, mate."

The pints were placed down in front of them. Chris picked his pint up with a shaking hand. Nick ordered two double shots of Jim Beam.

"You wanna sit down?"

Chris nodded again and Nick guided him over to a booth. He slid in next to him and placed the bourbon in front of him.

"Here, knock that back."

Chris did as instructed.

"Thanks."

"No worries, mate. You OK?"

"Me? Yeah, I'm fine. Just... you know."

"Yeah."

They both silently sipped their pints. Nick tried to think of something reassuring to say. But couldn't.

"You do this a lot?"

"What?"

"Pick up lads like me. For this fella?"

"It's amongst my many duties on occasion."

"Is he alright?"

"Yeah, he's OK."

"For a boss?"

"He's not exactly my boss."

"Really? Seems like it."

"Well, it's..."

"Complicated?"

"Extremely fucking so, kid. Come on, drink up and I'll drop you home."

"That's alright, I'm gonna stay out."

"That fifty quid burning a hole in your pocket?"

"A bit, yeah."

"Where you heading?"

"To the Krazy House, probably."

"I'll drop you there."

"No, it's fine. I fancy the walk."

"That's a long walk, mate. Not through the nicest part of town, either."

"I'll be fine."

"Why take the risk? Let me drop you."

"Really, I'll be fine."

"Alright then, if you insist."

Nick drained the last of his pint and stood up. He offered his hand, and Chris shook it.

"Look after yourself, Chris, was nice meeting you."

"You too."

Nick walked away but stopped as he got to the front doors of the hotel. He walked back into the bar and slid back into the booth next to Chris.

"I'm serious. Why take the risk?"

"What?"

"Why take the risk? Not just with walking through

town, but... this."

He gestured vaguely at the hotel lobby.

"Meeting strange men you don't know the first thing about on the internet. Meeting up with them to... do whatever you did. It's dangerous. That's all I'm saying. You're what, seventeen?"

"Eighteen."

"Eighteen. Fuck me, to be eighteen years old again. You're eighteen, you've got your whole life in front of you. You're a good-looking boy. *Really* good-looking. You don't need to be meeting old farts online. You could have your choice of boys, girls, whatever the fuck you want. You don't need to be doing this shit."

"This shit? Sorry, didn't you just come to my house to pick me up to do 'this shit'?"

"Yeah, OK, so I'm just a big fucking hypocrite. Fair enough. Look, I'm not judging you or anything. Don't get me wrong. All I'm saying is... oh, fuck, I don't know what I'm saying. You're right, I'm full of shit."

"No, you're not. I didn't mean to be a twat. You're alright. I appreciate what you're saying. Really."

Chris's hand dropped down from the table, onto Nick's thigh.

"You know, I wouldn't charge you."

Nick lifted Chris's hand off his thigh and back onto the table.

"If I was that way inclined, then I'd be the luckiest man in Liverpool right now. But that's what I'm talking about. Don't be putting yourself in these situations. Have a bit more respect for yourself. Right, I'm off. Maybe our paths will cross again at some point."

"Yeah, maybe. And thanks, Nick."

"I didn't actually do anything. But you're welcome."

Nick shook hands with Chris again and walked back to his car. He reached into his glove box and took out the blister pack of tablets. He popped a couple into his hand and swallowed them. He took a deep breath and turned the key in the ignition.

NINETEEN

"With regards to the alarm system, it's state-of-the-art. As long as it's used at all times, it'll keep the home secure."

James Powell nodded.

"It should do. It fucking cost enough."

"You can't put a price on your family's safety, James."

James's phone vibrated in his pocket. He took it out and silenced it.

"No? Well, you have, Nick. A big price. So what else should we be doing?"

There had been a spate of recent burglaries of footballers' homes in the area. Local gangs had targeted footballers' homes while the players were at away matches in different parts of the country or in Europe. The homes were mostly empty but, in one case two nights ago, a player's wife was at home and had been tied up and urinated on by the gang. Not a client of HTSS, of course. For Nick, this was all good news. He had significantly increased the number of accounts he had with footballers in the last couple of months. They were his favourite type of clients: they all had shit-loads of money and were mostly too stupid to know what to do with it, and could easily be talked into taking out the most costly deals. James Powell, centre-forward for Liverpool, was just the latest of them, and was the perfect example. Twenty-two years of age, just signed a new contract worth ninety grand a week, plus all the usual bonuses and add-ons. As far as Nick was concerned, the more burglary gangs there were operating around Liverpool, Cheshire and the Wirral, the better.

"Well, as you know, the main danger is when you're away with the team. Simple steps can make a big difference. For instance, if Katie is home alone, she should make sure everywhere is secured, and not answer the door to anyone other than expected people."

Nick's own phone rang loudly. He looked at the caller display and saw that it was Michael. He pressed to reject the call and put it back in his pocket.

"Also, you should be careful about your use of social-networking sites. For example, don't tweet that you're away in Marbella. Don't post Instagram pictures of you on a big night out. Things like that are just an open invitation to these gangs."

Nick's phone bleeped. He opened it up and saw the text message was from Michael. *Nick, I need to see you. My office. Twenty minutes.* He put the phone away and extended his hand to Powell. Powell offered his fist instead. Nick felt ridiculous – two white men, one of them middle-aged, giving each other a fist-bump – but whatever it took to keep the clients happy.

"Now, you've got my mobile number. I can be reached on that number pretty much anytime, day or night, so if you've got any further questions, don't hesitate to give me a call."

Nick fast-walked to the Evoque and started it up. The soft hum of the engine was drowned out by the Neil Young guitar solo blasting out from the stereo. He churned up some of the gravel on Powell's driveway as he spun around and gunned it out of there, heading back into town.

*

"I don't expect my calls to be rejected when I try to phone you, Nick."

"And a very good morning to you too, Michael."

"Don't be sarcastic, Nick. It's a form of humour I've always felt panders only to the lowest common denominator."

Nick sat down on the opposite side of Michael's huge desk. He held his hands up in surrender.

"Apologies."

"Joking apart, Nick, I called you over half an hour ago. I'm not accustomed to being kept waiting."

"I got here as quickly as I could. I was with a new

client."

Michael nodded his head.

"I understand. I'm a businessman, Nick. I understand how important it is to keep one's clients and associates happy. And I'm not an unreasonable man. Far from it. All I ask of you, Nick, is that, while you're keeping these clients of yours happy, just remember who it is that used his extensive network to establish your first group of clients, and who still regularly does so to keep that client list growing."

"Come on, Michael. You know how much I value you. Do I ever let you down?"

"Of course not, in fact I wanted to see you partly to thank you for your discreet work the other night. That package you brought me more than met my expectations."

Nick was unable to cover a wince.

"I'm sorry, Nick. I know you don't like me going into details like that. It's just that you're the only person who knows of my particular... tendencies. It's hard keeping your true self hidden, as you well know. I just need to unburden myself a little from time to time."

"I know, Michael. It's fine. You know I'm not one to judge anyone."

"Oh, I know. And nor do I judge you for your own personal indiscretions. What I'm trying to say, Nick, is that you and I, we have a very unique bond. A very special relationship. You've been invaluable to me over the years. And I like to think that I've been of great value to you."

"Of course."

"I just don't want you to lose sight of that. I'm not suggesting you have to drop everything as soon as I click my fingers. I just expect a certain amount of... special consideration."

Nick nodded his head.

"And this is a two-way street, Nick. I want you to know that I'm always available if you need to talk. I can see you've been a bit distracted lately. And judging by the size of your pupils I'm guessing you've been allowing some of those baser instincts we've talked about to take control. And, as I

110

say, I'm not judging. I just want you to know that I'm here for you. I know your birthday is coming up, and I know what a difficult time it is for you. Hence the smack, I dare say."

March, 1989. Nick turned onto his street on his bike, swigging from a can of Coke, steering with a single hand. He saw the police car parked on the street. He threw the can down, gripped the handle bars and pedalled harder. As he got close up to it, he realised it was definitely outside his house. He jumped off the bike and let it crash into the gatepost. He ran inside and into the living room to find his dad sitting on the couch, a can of lager in his hand, a WPC next to him, a male officer stood in front of the TV. The WPC stood up as Nick entered.

"I'm sorry, we've got some terribly sad news. Why don't you sit down?"

"Oh, fuck that," his dad said, rising up from the couch and throwing his can to the floor, "I'll tell him. She's gone, your mother. Gone"

"Gone? Gone where?"

"She's fucking dead! The cunt fucking killed herself, so you'd better get used to the idea. It's just me and you now."

"Nick, are you listening?"

Nick snapped back to the present day.

"Yes, sorry, Michael. I'm listening."

"This is what I'm talking about, Nick."

Michael stood up and walked round to Nick's side of the desk. He leaned over him and put his hands on his shoulders, put his face right in close.

"You need to get a hold of yourself, Nick. All the boozing and the drugs, they're fucking with your head." He tapped Nick's forehead hard with his finger as he said this. "They're not good for business. Now, go and sober the fuck up, or come down or whatever it is that you need to do. And I want to see you more focussed from here on in. You hear me, Nick?"

He took a deep breath and nodded his head.

"Loud and clear, Michael."

TWENTY

Scott closed his eyes. He pinched his thumbs and middle fingers together and breathed in a long, slow, steady breath through his nose, then slowly pushed it out through his mouth. He'd dreamt about him again, the boy from the Krazy House. He'd woken up hard, the image penetrating his post-sleep fogginess. He'd tried to lose the image. He smacked himself on the side of the head, punched himself in the temples trying to dislodge it, but that just intensified it in his mind; the face, those eyes, the thoughts of naked body parts. He couldn't get rid. They wouldn't leave him alone. *He* wouldn't leave him alone. The fucking boy. He wouldn't leave him in peace. Scott didn't know how it had happened, but he had gotten inside his head. That night in the Krazy House, when he saw him near the dance floor, when the boy *fucking smiled* at him, something had happened. Something had passed between them. It was like he'd cast some fucking spell over him or something.

He jumped out of bed and got straight down onto the floor and sat cross-legged. As he closed his eyes he saw the boy's face again. He forced his eyes closed again and began breathing slowly in and out. He silently repeated his mantra over and over. Mitch had recommended some words for him to use – today he was using "serene". Mitch had told him it needn't matter which word he used, but to use words like "calm", "serene" and "peace" would be ideal for Scott's stated need to use meditation as a form of anger management. He'd been taking it really seriously, and had gone to every Thursday-evening session for the last few weeks, and a couple of Wednesday-morning sessions too. He had also been doing it at home daily – sometimes three or four times a day. He was approaching it with the same degree of dedication and intensity he applied to his workouts. That's how he had come to see the meditation: a mental workout. His body was taken care of at the gym, his mind was taken care of through meditation. He intoned his mantra for the day over and over, and finally the images dispersed. The boy was gone.

*

Another set of fifty reps on the lat pulldown, followed by five sets of fifty shoulder lifts, then ten sets of one hundred bench presses. After that, he'd finish off with a twenty-minute run and then he'd hit the sauna, where he would meditate again. Today he was meeting Carrie. He had agreed to see a Relate counsellor with her, and today was their first meeting or session or whatever they called it, and he was nervous about it. He had no idea what to expect, so he wanted to be as mentally prepared as possible; he figured it could only help if Carrie could pick up on how much the meditation was helping him, how much it was changing him. And of course, he wanted to be looking his best for her.

*

"So, today's session will start off as a getting-to-know-you kind of chat, which will give me a chance to get a sense of where you are in your relationship."

Scott took an instant dislike to Phillip, the counsellor. He took an instant dislike to his name, to his preppy tie and V-neck look, to his fucking hipster-looking, thick-rimmed glasses, to his neatly-trimmed, designer fucking stubble. If this cunt was to try and get into a club where Scott was working the door, he'd refuse him entry just for a laugh. Just to wipe that smug, self-satisfied fucking look off his face, and just to see how fucking pathetically helpless he'd be, how he'd try and use smart-arsed words to talk his way in, and to see how uselessly fucking impotent he'd be. That was another thing Scott loved about his work – getting to turn the tables on people who obviously thought they were hot shit in their worlds. But, for now, he'd have to try and keep a lid on it, be tolerant at least, just say the right things and get through these sessions.

"For starters, why don't you tell me a bit about your

lives together? Carrie, why don't you start?"

"Well, we'd been, or have been, together for about three years now," she said, nervously fiddling with a tissue in her hands.

"And how did you meet?"

"I used to go to a club where Scott worked. I'd noticed him a few times, and always thought he was really good-looking. We got talking to each other over a few months."

"Who initiated the interaction between you?"

"That was probably Scott, mostly."

Scott nodded his head in agreement.

"So Scott asked you out? Then what happened?"

"First we went out on a couple of dates. Nothing special, just meeting for a drink. One time we went out for dinner."

"And what were you impressions of Scott?"

"He was nice. He always acted like a gentleman. He held doors open for me, never let me pay for anything."

"And how did your relationship progress from there?"

"Quickly," she said, still fiddling with the tissue. "We started seeing each other three or four times a week, then soon it was most days. I'd end up staying over at his flat for about half the week. After about six weeks or so, I pretty much moved in."

"OK, thank you for that, Carrie. Scott, why don't you give me your impression of the early days of your relationship?"

Scott shrugged his shoulders.

"Pretty much how she tells it."

He noticed her turn her head sideways to look at him. He felt her eyes burrowing into him, and she didn't need to verbalise her objections. He had promised to engage with this process and here he was already being dismissive and uncooperative at the first question. He took a deep breath and continued.

"I really liked her straight from the off. I mean, she's gorgeous, that's obvious. But there was much more to it than that, even right at the start. Even before I'd spoken to her, I knew she was special, like. Sometimes, you can just tell with people. And that's how it was with Carrie."

He stopped for a moment, as it hit him once again how much he loved Carrie, and it threatened to overwhelm him. He noticed she had started to sob very quietly. He went on.

"As she said, things moved along very quickly. I'd never had a serious girlfriend before, I'd always preferred being single, but with Carrie, I wanted it to be serious. And I was so glad when she moved in with me."

"Did you ask Carrie to move in?"

"No, not really. It just sort of happened over a few weeks. We never really talked about it. It just sort of happened naturally."

"So that was about three years ago. So what exactly is it that's brought you both here today?"

Scott looked away, and Phillip knew well enough when someone was ready or not to talk, so he turned to Carrie.

"Carrie?"

"Well, we've been having a bit of trouble. A few weeks ago – " She paused, and started fiddling with the tissue even more. "A few weeks ago, well, Scott hit me."

"I see."

"I mean, it wasn't hard. It wasn't like a punch or anything. It was just a slap."

"And what happened leading up to that?"

They both hesitated this time. Scott decided to speak.

"We'd been arguing a bit."

"And what were you arguing about?"

Scott turned away and looked at the wall again. He couldn't bring himself to say the next part.

"Sex," Carrie said very quietly. Scott's fists clenched involuntarily.

"Please go on."

"We'd been arguing about sex. You see," she pulled at the tissue, "Scott's tastes had changed a bit. For the last year or so, the only kind of sex he was interested in was anal. And I didn't mind trying it a few times, but it got so that's all he was interested in."

Scott's fists were balled so tight his knuckles were white.

"And when we did that," she continued, "he was totally different."

"In what way?"

"Well, when we did it in the... in the front, he was always really gentle in bed. Really tender, you know? But when we did... that, he was just so rough." The tissue was now shredded in her hands, bits of it falling to the floor. "And he used to always look me right in the eyes while we made love. But when we did anal, he'd always want the light off, and he was just so... rough with me. It was like being with a different person. A person who didn't seem to care very much about me or how I felt."

Scott stood up, knocking his chair over.

"This is too much, Carrie. I know I said I'd try, but this is way too much. Why do I have to sit here and listen to myself being slagged off like this? It's personal, we don't need someone else telling us what to say and do, finding out the most private things about us. We can work through this ourselves."

"Scott," Phillip said, "nobody is slagging anybody off, that's not what this is about. What this is, is an opportunity for everyone to get everything out in the open. This is a safe environment for *both* of you to get everything out there. There's no judgement in here, Scott. And you'll have your chance to offer your perspective on everything soon too."

Scott was surprised to feel himself calming down. At first he had wanted to smash the specky little fucker's face into the wall, but he had managed to talk him round. He was obviously good at what he did. Scott lifted his chair up and slowly sat back down.

"I'm sorry about that," he said.

"It's fine, Scott. Why don't you take the opportunity to tell me, in your own words, how you felt leading up to the moment when you hit Carrie."

And he did. For a further forty minutes, he talked, and he listened to Carrie, and he listened to Phillip. He listened to Carrie talk about his steroid use, about his mood swings in the months leading up to the slap. For her, everything changed when his steroid use increased. The fixation with anal sex began then also. He talked about the day he hit her, how tired he'd been after pulling a long and busy shift in Manchester and driving back to Liverpool in the early hours, going straight to the gym, and being plain exhausted when Carrie chose the worst possible time to speak to him about the sex and the moods. She accepted that she had approached the issue all wrong; Scott stated how he felt like he was being attacked, like he had been backed into a corner, and for one split second, he lost control and lashed out, instantly regretting what he'd done.

At the end of the session, they were both spent, but each felt like some progress had been made, and Phillip assured them that it had been a very positive first session. They walked outside together, and Scott tried to hold her hand. She let him, but didn't really hold his hand back, more allowing hers to rest in his.

"Can I give you a lift back to your mam's?"

"No, it's fine, I'll get the train."

"Come home, Carrie. Come back to the house with me."

"No, I can't."

"Why not? You agreed we'd made some progress. Phillip said how well we'd both done."

"I know, but it's not that easy. We can't just get straight back together after one session. It's gonna take time, Scott."

"How much time?" Scott asked, now holding both her hands in his.

"I don't know, Scott. You can't pressure me like this. You have to be patient."

She gently prised her hands from his. He nodded his head.

"OK," he said. He pulled her close and held her tight.

This time he felt her resistance lessen, and she eventually put her arms around his waist. "I'm not gonna give up, you know. I love you too much." She didn't say anything, but she nodded, and he knew she understood.

She said goodbye and he watched her walk in the direction of Liverpool Central. He closed his eyes and silently repeated "serene, serene, serene" over and over in his head.

TWENTY-ONE

Nick turned over in his sleep. His eyes opened slowly, and he saw Francis was lying there next to him.

"What the fuck are you doing here?" Nick asked him.

"You're the private detective, aren't you? Like Shaft." Francis strummed an imaginary guitar and made wah-wah sounds. "Or whatever it is you do, you tell me."

"You shouldn't be here, Francis. It's not right. This is where I live. This is my home. I think you'd better leave."

"But I haven't got anywhere else to go."

"That's not my problem."

"Oh, I'd beg to differ, good sir. It was you that brought me here. It's not like I asked to come, is it?"

"Just fuck off, Francis. This is the third time you've turned up like this."

"OK. I'll go, but only if you promise to come and visit me soon, Nick."

"I dunno, Francis. I never really liked you all that much when you were alive, to be honest. You always talked like some fucking street poet or something. Always did my fucking head in."

Nick felt a pushing at his back.

"Nick. Nick, wake up."

He sat up, wiping away some congealed drool from the corner of his mouth. He looked around and saw Kathleen, her hand on his shoulder, a cup of coffee in her other hand.

"Nick, you were talking in your sleep."

"Fuck, was I? Nothing incriminating, I hope?"

"Well, you were telling someone to fuck off. The rest of it was pretty much unintelligible. Is everything OK?"

"Yeah, I'm fine. Just a bit tired is all. Been working hard, you know?"

"Of course I know. I see how hard you're working yourself," she said as she sat down opposite. "Will you not think about hiring someone? The amount of clients you've added this last year, no one man can possibly keep on top of them all. And it's not like you can't afford it. The money you're bringing in, you could easily hire one full-time or two part-time assistants. Please, Nick, you'll burn out if you don't."

Nick was already shaking his head before she had even finished speaking.

"No. Absolutely not. No assistants. I've got Danny and Sam for when I need help, I'm not taking on anyone permanent."

"Why not?"

"I like to be hands-on. I wouldn't trust anyone else to do any of the work. And that's what most of the clients like: knowing it's always gonna be me on the end of the phone, not some spotty kid or someone in a call centre."

"But, Nick, you're falling asleep at your desk. What if it had been while you were driving?"

"Look, I'm fine. Really, you don't have to worry about me."

He pointed to the coffee.

"Is that for me?"

Kathleen nodded and left the office. Nick took a big swig of the coffee and rubbed his eyes. He opened his desk drawer and took out a small square mirror with some coke and a razor blade on it. He cut up a nice, fat line and snorted it up. He rubbed a bit into his gums and cut another line. Halfway along the line he caught sight of the clock on his desk. 15:23.

"Fuck," he said. "Fuck, fuck, fuck."

He jumped up from his desk and grabbed his car keys and ran for the door. As he got there he stopped and ran back to his desk and pushed the mirror into the drawer and ran through the outer office.

"Fuck, fuck, fuck."

"What is it, Nick?"

"I was meant to pick Monica up from school ten

120

fucking minutes ago."

"Oh no."

"Do me a favour, phone the school, tell them I'm stuck in traffic but that I'm on my way."

"OK, but please drive carefully."

He took the lift down to the parking level and drove out of there like Batman out of the Batcave, nearly hitting someone as he did. He slalomed in and out of traffic, receiving angry beeps and V signs. He sped away from traffic lights, and a couple he didn't even stop at. He completed a fifteen-minute drive in less than ten, and skidded to a halt outside the school. He ran inside to find Monica sitting in the head's office, doodling in a colouring book. He apologised profusely to the head and carried Monica, who didn't seem to have noticed anything was wrong, out to the car. He took a deep breath before he turned the key in the ignition, and drove calmly out of the gate.

The drive towards home was a much more sedate affair than the drive to school. He chatted with Monica about her day, him looking at her in his rear-view mirror, her looking out of the window with that keen curiosity she always had in her eyes.

"Have you had a nice day at school, munchkin?"

"Yes," she answered.

"What did you do?"

"We did PE in the morning, then did maths. After that, is was lunchtime."

"Did you get all your sums right?"

"Not all of them but I got lots of them right."

"What a clever girl. And who did you sit with at lunchtime?"

"I sat with Cerys, Lottie and Jessie, and we had roast dinner."

"Roast dinner? That's daddy's favourite. Did you save any for me?"

"No, I ate it all up!"

"What?" Nick said, turning round to face her. "You didn't save me any? Poor Daddy."

CRASH.

"Oh shit," Nick said as he felt the impact. He turned round to see that he'd gone into the back of the car in front. "Shit, shit, shit."

"You swore, Daddy."

"Just be quiet a minute, darling. Daddy just has to go and speak to this other driver for a minute. You just wait here."

Nick jumped out of the car. He was out before the other driver, and quickly checked for damage. There wasn't too much of it, just broken brake-lights on the other car, the front lights on his. Superficial damage, but he thought of the police, he thought of the coke in his system. If he got breathalysed he'd be fucked. The other driver got out, he was a man about Nick's age. Nick held his hands up.

"I'm so sorry about that, mate."

The man looked at his car's rear end.

"Well, there's not too much damage." Nick was relieved he wasn't being unreasonable. "What the hell happened?"

"It was my little girl, she was upset about something, I turned round for a second, no more, but that was all it took. Are you OK?"

"Yeah, I'm fine, don't worry about that. We'll have to swap insurance details."

"Well, here's the thing, mate. If we do this through my insurance, my premiums are gonna go through the roof, you know what I mean? Is there any chance we can just settle it by ourselves, you know, leave the insurance companies out of it, like?"

"Oh, I dunno about that, mate, I mean, we should really report the accident, shouldn't we?"

"No, no, no. There's no need for that, not for a little dink like this. Here," he took out his wallet and started peeling notes off. "This'll more than cover the cost of getting your lights fixed, and here's a bit extra just for being so understanding. You can get a full valet while you're getting them fixed."

The man stared at the thick, growing wad of cash Nick was now holding.

"Well, I suppose we can just leave it between ourselves then, I mean, if it's gonna affect your premiums and what-have-you."

"Thanks a lot, I really appreciate it. Here, take a card too."

He passed the man a card. He took it and read it.

"'Hanman Total Security Solutions. Security Consultancy'. Erm, I'm not sure I'd have much call to use a security consultant."

"Well, if you ever do, I'd sort you out with a nice discount anyway. Thanks again for being so understanding," he said, shaking the man's hand and turning back towards his car.

"Is the car broken, Daddy?" Monica asked as he got back in and closed the door.

"No, munchkin, the car's fine. Listen, darling, don't say anything to Mummy about this, OK?"

"Why not?"

"Well, it'd just make Mummy worry and get upset if you told her. You wouldn't want Mummy to get upset now, would you?"

"No, I suppose not."

"So we can just keep it as our little secret, then, can't we?"

"OK."

"That's my girl."

TWENTY-TWO

This was it. This was going to be the day when it all changed. After weeks of regular meditation, regular Relate sessions and a few "dates" he thought had gone pretty well, Carrie had texted him asking for him to come round for a talk. This was the first time she had invited him to her mum and dad's since she'd moved back in there, so it had to be something big. He was so excited he had woken up at half-six, done over a thousand crunches, five hundred push-ups and ten sets of fifty shoulder lifts with his dumbbells. He followed it with a jog around the park before hitting the shower, shaving and having breakfast.

He put on the Armani T-shirt he'd spent a few days' worth of wages on, with his Diesel jeans and his new Adidas trainers. He stood in front of the mirror. He looked so fucking good right now. Almost as good as he felt. He realised he had probably not stopped smiling since he'd received her text last night. He knew it wasn't good to get too carried away, but he couldn't help it. He had spoken briefly to Mitch after last night's session, who had told him how important it is to have a positive mind-set, and how that mind-set can feed into your body language and vice-versa, and how creating a positive aura around yourself can actually alter how those around you thought and acted. Just a few weeks ago, Scott would have laughed out loud if someone had said something like that to him. But now, having exposed himself to this way of thinking, he could actually believe it. And if it was true, then the positive vibes he was feeling now could only help his cause.

*

Scott knocked on the door and stole a last-minute check of his complexion in the window, and smelled the half-dozen roses he'd bought. Carrie answered the door. He was surprised she was wearing tracksuit bottoms and a T-shirt, her hair scraped back into a tight ponytail, with no makeup. He suddenly felt self-conscious for having made such an effort, but he quickly told himself it wasn't important how she was dressed. What mattered was what was about to happen – the rebirth of their relationship.

"Hiya," he said. "I got these for you."

He held out the flowers to her.

"You... you shouldn't have," she said, and stared at them for a time that was brief, but enough to make him feel a bit awkward. Eventually, she took them from him and stepped aside to let him enter.

"Your folks home?"

"No, they've gone out. Go through to the living room."

He stepped past her and into the living room. He turned around to speak but Carrie wasn't there. She came in minus the flowers.

They both attempted to speak at the same time. He laughed and invited her to speak first.

"No, go on. You first."

"Carrie, I just wanted to say, these last few weeks have been great. It's been like when we first got together. So exciting. And I've changed so much, too. And I feel like we've changed together, and we're gonna grow so much together in the future – "

He stopped talking when she lowered her head and rubbed at her forehead with her right hand.

"Are you OK, babes? You got a headache or something?"

"No, it's not that."

"What, then?"

"Look Scott, I... there's no way to say this," he felt his heart sink, "but we're not gonna be getting back together."

He almost vomited on the spot. His guts clenched painfully and he broke out in an instant cold sweat.

"What? Wh-why?"

She didn't say anything.

"Carrie, why? Why? I've... I've done everything you

asked. I've stopped the steroids. I've been going to meditation. I mean I've really got into the meditation. I never thought I would but I have. Carrie, please, talk to me. Say something."

"I'm sorry," she said, crying now.

"Don't be sorry, tell me why. Can't you see how hard I've tried?"

"I know you've tried," she managed to say through the tears, "I know. You've tried so hard."

"Well what is it, then?"

"It's just..." She trailed off.

"Please, Carrie." He tried to put his hand on her arm but she pulled away from him. "I'm sorry for what I did. You know I am. That's why I've done everything I have."

"I know you're sorry, and it's not that. I forgive you for that."

"Then what? For fuck's sake, if you've forgiven me for that, and you can see all the changes I've made, then what else is there?" He felt the rage building, and took a moment to try and compose himself. "It must be enough that we love each other. You do love me, don't you?"

She burst into larger tears, and held her head in both hands.

"I'm so sorry." He could barely make out what she was saying.

"Carrie, do you love me?"

She shook her head from side to side.

"I'm so sorry," she said again, "but I don't. Not like that. Not anymore."

He felt himself go light-headed and put his hand against the wall to steady himself.

"I can't believe it. I really thought you'd invited me round to say you were gonna move back in with me. I don't know what to say. Is that it? Is there any chance?"

She shook her head again and began to regain some of her composure.

"No. I have to be honest with you now. That's what Phillip said. I went for a session with him the other day, and he told me we have to be totally honest with each other now, so that there can't be any misunderstandings."

"Is this down to him? Has that little bastard... has he said something to you? I could tell he didn't like me from the start, the fucking little nerd. It's all down to him, isn't it?"

"It's nothing to do with him!" Scott was taken aback by her raised voice. "I know my own mind, Scott. I know what I want and what I think. I just went to him for help in breaking it to you. I'm sorry, Scott, but there's no chance. I'm sorry but I don't love you anymore. I care about you, very much, and I want you to be happy, but that's not gonna be with me. And I'm leaving Liverpool."

"What?"

"You remember my aunty Eileen who lives in Dublin? Well I'm gonna move in with her for a bit and find a job out there. I'm gonna start again, Scott, and I suggest that you do the same."

"I'm not moving to Ireland."

"I mean you should start again. Start over."

He laughed at the stupid misunderstanding. He felt like such an idiot. He looked at the clothes he'd bought. He thought of the speeches he'd practised, the roses he'd bought, and he thought of what a fucking idiot he'd been. He felt his pulse racing. He tried to do some breathing exercises to calm himself down, but it was no good. He'd been humiliated. He felt such a fool.

"I'm so sorr—"

He didn't let her finish. He grabbed her by the throat and lifted her effortlessly off the floor. He held her against the wall with one hand, the other one clenching. He squeezed her throat. She tried to loosen his grip but she didn't stand a chance against his strength. She tried to speak, but her face was now turning purple, her eyes rolling back in her head. He lifted his fist right up in front of her face. He drew his fist back and held it there, then slammed it into the wall next to her face. He pulled it back and did it again. And again. He finally let go of her and she dropped to the floor by his feet, coughing and gasping for breath. He slammed his fist into the wall again and again. Chunks of plaster fell from it onto the floor. He didn't stop punching until his hand was gushing blood and he heard bones in his hand shatter. He didn't even look at her, he turned and left the living room and grabbed the roses as he headed to the front door. He threw them into the bin outside the house as he left.

TWENTY-THREE

"Wake up, you bastard."

Nick wasn't sure which brought him round first – the shouting or the glass of water that was simultaneously thrown over him. He sat bolt upright in bed to see Lisa standing beside it.

"What the fuck are you doing?" he shouted.

"You bastard. You fucking bastard."

"What? What have I done?"

"You fucking know."

"I don't. What the fuck have I done?"

In truth, he knew the list of things he had done was a long one; Lisa could have been talking about any one of dozens of things.

"Well you wouldn't know because you were completely comatose last night, but Monica was awake half the night having nightmares. Nightmares about being in a car crash."

His face must have betrayed him.

"That's right. Now you fucking know, don't you? Then this morning she says she doesn't want to get into the car in case we crash. It took me ten minutes to calm her down enough to get her in the car. Then on the drive she tells me about your crash the other day, and how she isn't supposed to tell me because it's a secret. Getting your four-year-old daughter to lie so you can try and cover your own arse. That's a new low even for you, Nick. Then I find out from the school that you were half an hour late picking her up on Friday. So what was it, Nick? Were you drunk or on drugs?"

"Lisa, look... I..."

"You what? I hope you're not going to try and deny it now."

"No, I'm not. It's not how you think, it was just a little dink, could have happened to anyone."

"But it didn't, it happened to you, didn't it? And while our daughter was in the car with you. And no doubt while you're either pissed or off your head on something. And then you get her to lie for you."

"It was just... I didn't wanna worry you, that's all."

"Bullshit. You were trying to cover your arse."

"No – "

"Yes. You're a fucking coward."

He couldn't bring himself to deny this, as he knew it was one of those truths that were self-evident.

"Please, Lisa."

"No. It's too late."

She walked to the closet and pulled a suitcase off the shelf and threw it onto the bed.

"I want you out of this house."

"Come on, Lisa, it was just a little crash, you can't throw me out over that."

"It's not just that, though, is it, Nick? This is just the final straw. It's everything. It's the drink. It's the drugs. It's the secrecy. It's the God knows what you do for your job."

"You can't use that against me. We've talked about this before. We always agreed that what I did for work would be my business only. That you wouldn't ask questions."

"Yes, we did. But that was as long as you left it outside of this house, but you can't keep the two separate anymore. You're bringing it home with you. You've been bringing it home for a long time. Now it's putting our daughter in danger, and I'm not having it."

He got up and out of bed.

"Lisa, please, come on. It doesn't have to be like this."

"It does, Nick. Until you can sort your head out, this is exactly how it has to be. I won't expose our daughter or myself to the poison you bring into this house any longer."

He dropped to his knees in tears.

"Please, Lisa. I love you. I adore Monica. I just... I can't..."

"You can't what, Nick? You can't leave the drink, the drugs? You love those things more than me and Monica?"

"No, of course I don't."

"They're not even the worst thing, Nick. I could have dealt with that if you hadn't dragged Monica into it. The worst thing is how emotionally absent you are. You're more dedicated to Michael Epson than you are to us."

"That's not true."

"But it is true, Nick. Even when you're here, you might as well not be. Your mind is constantly elsewhere. You'll drop us like a hot stone the second you get the signal from him. You're in thrall to him. And you're in thrall to your father as well. That monster of a man, who abused you for all those years, who is still abusing you now. And who'll never stop abusing you. Him and Epson, they're like ghosts in this house, they lurk at the back of everything you do."

He wasn't even crying anymore. He just nodded along with everything Lisa said. Because he knew it was all true. He didn't have the strength to deny it or argue it anymore.

"Please, Lisa. Don't give up on me."

"Don't you dare do that. Don't turn this around on me. I've tried to help you, tried to reach you, but you're just too far gone. You can't be reached."

Again he just nodded along.

"I'm going out, and I want you gone by the time I get back, Nick. And don't come back until you've cleaned yourself up, and until you're ready to deal with all this shit. And I mean properly. Not a few weeks of sobriety before the inevitable relapse. And, most of all, I want you to deal with your dad and Epson."

Without another word, she turned and left.

He stayed kneeling on the floor for a few minutes, in a state of shock. He heard his phone ring. He picked it up and saw Michael Epson's name on the caller display. He threw the phone across the room and began packing his suitcase.

*

Mitch shook hands with the last few members of the group as they left the hall, and received a few pats on the back.

"Cheers... good to see ya... see ya next week," he said to various group members. Tonight's session had been a really good one. There was a really positive vibe going round the group, even more so than usual. He walked back over to his mat and sat down, crossed-legged. After a session, he always liked to take five minutes to himself, just to reflect on how the session had gone, and to realign his thinking. He crossed his eyes and sat there for a good ten or fifteen minutes, just soaking up the positive ambience that was still in the room.

He stood up and rolled his mat away, put his shoes and socks back on and switched out the lights. He closed the door to the hall and put the padlock on. He turned round and saw a dark figure standing in front of him. Before he could tell who it was he was punched, and punched hard, right in the face. He dropped to his knees, his hand covering where he'd been hit. He began to look upwards, but received a second, even harder, punch to the face. This time he dropped to his hands and knees, blinded by his watering eyes and blood from his nose. Then he felt a much heavier blow, too heavy to be a punch or a kick, maybe a brick or a rock, to the back of his head. A deafening ringing sound instantly filled his ears. He tried to stand, reaching out for the door or the wall to steady himself with, but his legs couldn't bear his weight, so he went down on his knees again. He couldn't see a thing, but what was unmistakeably a kick went into his guts, followed by another heavy blow to the side of his head. This time he was knocked prone onto the floor. He could hear the heavy breathing of his attacker as he leaned in close to him.

"You fucking liar," he said.

Then everything went black.

TWENTY-FOUR

"Hi, can I buy you a drink?"

"Of course you can," Chris said, "as long as you then leave me the fuck alone."

"Stuck-up little twink."

The man walked away. Chris knew he'd been mean, and he felt a bit bad about it, but he was so sick of these ugly old queens cruising him. The old part he was OK with, but the ugly queen part he was definitely not cool with. He was looking for *men,* not these mincing old poofs. He'd been in a bunch of Liverpool's many gay clubs and bars every night in the last week, and the best he had managed was a few snog-and-grope sessions with a few pretty-boys. He'd let one of them wank him off in a dark corner of one club, but it wasn't what he was looking for. He was hoping he'd see the guy whose cock he had sucked in The Curzon but he was nowhere to be seen, and nor were any viable alternatives. He turned his bar stool around so he could give the club a last scan. Still he saw no one he'd be interested in. He downed the rest of his drink and headed towards the door. Just before he reached it, yet another old queen stepped in front of him.

"Not leaving already, are you?" he asked.

Chris looked him up and down.

"Look at you and look at me. Do you honestly think you've got any chance?"

"Oh, suit yourself, then," the man said, turning back to his friends.

"I intend to."

*

"So what the fuck happened to it?"

"Well, I was cleaning the car and when I'd been inside it I must have knocked the handbrake off or something

133

coz when I was cleaning the hubcaps it just started rolling backwards, and I tried to stop it but managed to get my hand run over."

"Fucking hell, Scotty, lad, that's bad."

"I know," he said, holding up his hand, now heavily bandaged. "Didn't half hurt. Amazing, the ways you can manage to hurt yourself."

"How badly damaged is it?" Kev asked.

"Not as bad as it could have been. Mainly knuckle damage. Will have to keep this on for a while, like."

Kev shook his head gravely.

"Fucking hell. I hope that's not your wanking hand. Evening, ladies," he said as a couple of short-skirt-wearing young things approached the door of Revolution. "You have a good night, girls."

He turned to Scott.

"Fucking hell," he said, "did you see them two? Tell you what, give them an hour to get themselves drunk enough and I'll be up to me nuts in guts with them."

Scott forced himself to laugh and say something in agreement. His mind wasn't focussed on work at all tonight, and he had no interest in perving on some stupid fucking young bitches. He was now off women. Fuck them. Fuck them all. Fucking cock-teasing, lying head-fuckers, all of them. He knew what he wanted and it sure as fuck wasn't women. But he had to keep up the pretence, at least until he could get a hold of the thoughts he was having and find some way to control them. He had decided he had to keep himself busy; the more time he had to think, the more those thoughts got a foothold. So he had decided to throw himself into work.

This was the first shift he'd done since he'd seen Carrie. Since then, everything had been turned upside down. The only times he'd left the house before tonight were to have some marathon sessions in the gym. He'd spent over three hours there the day after he'd seen her, then four hours the next day, then close to five hours the day after that, all the time ignoring the pain from his damaged fingers and knuckles. In fact he welcomed the pain. It gave him another thing to focus his mind on, and he had been taking more coke as well, which helped, along with the Tramadol he'd been prescribed. He'd dispensed with the meditation completely. Never again would he use that fucking hippy bollocks. From now on he was gonna do things his own way. It was gonna be work and the gym all the way. The meditation had been for Carrie, and now, with her gone, he had no use for it. And he was back into the steroids too. He'd actually started to reduce them when he thought he was getting back with Carrie – now he could take whatever he wanted, without that slag moaning to him. He'd taken forty milligrams of Dianabol after each gym session, and had managed to get his hands on some Androne Testosterone, which he'd been injecting into his arse. He was drinking gallons of protein shakes too. He was keeping himself busy now. And he wasn't missing that cunt Carrie at all. Good fucking riddance to her. In fact, if he could speak to her now, he'd thank her. Thank her for fucking off and leaving him to get on with his life. She was just holding him back. He was free now. He could do whatever the fuck he wanted and it didn't matter.

"You want a brew, mate?" Kev asked.

"Yeah, go on, then."

Kev picked up their mugs off the floor and headed inside. Scott turned away from the door and walked out to the edge of the steps and looked out on all the revellers heading in various directions, moving from one club to the next, some of them falling over in the street, already pissed. Shouting to or at each other across the street. It was then that he saw him. He was on the opposite side of the street, heading in his direction. The boy. The one he'd seen in the Krazy House that night. The one who had somehow managed to insert himself into Scott's dreams. He was there. And he was walking towards him. Everyone else on the street vanished for a moment, leaving just Scott – and him. A cold sweat ran down his back as the boy drew level with him, no more than twenty yards away from him now. Scott wasn't sure what he'd do if he now crossed the road and headed into Revolution. But he didn't cross over. He kept on walking. Scott watched him. He headed on down the road, then crossed over and headed in the direction of the Malaga Bar. A queer bar. He knew it. The boy was a faggot. That explained it. That explained why he was inserting himself into Scott's thoughts, into his dreams. It all made sense now. And he knew what he had to do.

*

"Come on everyone, out you go. Do your talking while you're walking."

The last few stragglers made their way reluctantly out of the doors of Revolution. They went their separate ways, in groups and on their own. To go home, to bed, to sleep or to fuck, on to whichever club would still let them in, to get kebabs and taxis, to find someone to fight.

"You coming for a bite to eat, Scott?" Steve asked.

"Nah, I don't think I will tonight, lads. I'm pretty knackered so I'm just gonna head home."

"Alright, take it easy, mate."

Scott hung deliberately back and let them all get a head-start on him. He waited until they were all out of sight, then slowly counted to one hundred. Then he walked down the Revolution steps and turned left. He walked very slowly, checking around him for anyone who might know him. He stopped opposite the Malaga and took his phone out of his pocket. He pretended to be texting, but he was really watching the door of the bar. He put his phone back in his pocket and checked the street, first to his left, then to his right.

He crossed the street.

TWENTY-FIVE

Buster had seen better days. His hips were inflamed and Miranda had to crush up arthritis medication and put it into his food. He had a permanent limp in his back legs from where he'd been hit by a car a few years ago. He was nearly blind in one eye and his hearing was shot. Regardless, every morning at six, Miranda took him for his morning walk and, once he was off the lead, he seemed to forget his multiple impairments. He bounced around the woods and chased the squirrels, he tore in and out of the trees, jumped into the lake and chased other dogs.

Miranda tried to keep up with him but she had a dodgy hip herself and didn't think it was fair to inhibit what was his greatest pleasure by keeping him on the lead, so she let him run where he wanted, keeping him in sight as much as she could without running herself. She had learned it was pointless calling him when he went too far out of sight. His hearing wasn't good enough to hear her, but when she'd completely lost track of him, she employed the use of a dog whistle, and he nearly always came running for that.

He had been out of sight for a good five minutes or so, so Miranda decided it was time to employ the whistle. She blew it and waited for a moment, expecting him to come lolloping out of the trees, but nothing. She kept walking in roughly the direction in which he had run off and blew it again. Still he didn't come, but she could hear a distant barking. She followed the sound and blew again. She was closing in on the sound of the barking now. The knowledge of the inherent futility of calling for a mostly deaf dog by name didn't stop her from doing just that. Of course, it didn't help, but she could now see his back end through a clearing in the trees.

"Buster, come here. Buster."

He had his face buried in something, what looked like a pile of leaves. She took a few steps closer and she realised it wasn't leaves; what she could see was a leg. At first she thought it was a mannequin, her initial impression not allowing for the obvious question of what a mannequin would be doing out here. Then she thought it was a sleeping homeless person, but realised that there was no way anyone could have slept through Buster's barking and her shouting. Gradually, the realisation hit her. She now knew what it was, without even seeing more than the leg. She approached cautiously now, and, when she got closer, she knew that what she saw would haunt her for the rest of her life.

It was the naked body of a man, lying on its back. The face had been battered so badly it hardly looked like a face at all. The torso looked like it was covered in one huge bruise, though Miranda couldn't be sure if it was just turning blue from the cold.

"Help," Miranda shouted, "somebody, please help."

She suddenly remembered all those detective shows she watched, remembered lines about not disturbing a crime scene, so she quickly put Buster on his lead and carefully stepped backwards away from the body. She crept away slowly until she was out of the tress, and ran as fast as she could back towards her car to call the police.

*

Around the time Merseyside Police were assembling their scene-of-crime tents around the body that had been found that morning, Nick Hanman was sitting in the Original Bistro in town eating brunch. He sat in the booth in the corner furthest away from the door, half-heartedly picking at some scrambled eggs, drinking another refill of his coffee and flicking through the paper. The noise of a family entering the café made him look up briefly, but long enough to see the family of four. Mum, a girl about eight and a boy about Monica's age, and the dad. The dad looked up and locked eyes with Nick for the briefest moment before Nick looked back up and did a double-take of the dad, who did the same with Nick before quickly

138

looking away again as his family piled into a booth five or six down from Nick. As he lowered himself into his seat, he took another glance in Nick's direction. He no doubt thought he was being discreet, but to Nick it was obvious, and all the confirmation Nick needed that this guy was indeed who Nick had thought he was.

Nick was nine years old. Steven Dunne was ten, nearly eleven, and in the year above him at school. For weeks now, Steven had been picking on Nick. Nothing much at first, just the usual playground shit, mostly. It started with Steven making jokes about Nick's scar. Then tripping him up in the corridor. But a week or so ago Steven had cornered Nick round the side of the school at break time. It had been building up recently, Steven seeming emboldened by Nick's lack of fighting back, and that day he seemed determined to move his bullying up a notch. Surrounded by his friends, he'd given Nick much more of a beating than usual. Instead of the usual punches to the stomach, today it was a kick to the bollocks and a couple of full-on punches to the face. These left Nick with a black eye which, unlike punches to the stomach, couldn't be hidden from his dad. When he got home, his dad had demanded to know the name of the boy and where he lived. John marched his son round there, Nick mortified at the idea of his dad knocking on the door and "telling on" Steven to his parents. When they got near the house, though, John suddenly stopped and held Nick back, a few doors down from Steven's. He leant against a wall, looking in the direction of the house. Nick was confused, but too scared to ask what was going on. After a while, though, he plucked up the courage to ask.

"What are we doing, Dad?"

"Waiting."

After nearly an hour, their wait was over. Steven left the house and started walking in the direction of the shops.

"That him?" John asked. Nick nodded his head and followed his dad as he set off after Steven.

"Oi!" John shouted and Steven stopped and looked around. He looked from John to Nick, fear registering in his

eyes but the usual arrogant bravado on his face. "You the prick who's been beating my lad up?"

Steven shrugged his shoulders slightly. Nick's heart was pounding. He wasn't sure what he felt, whether it was fear of what his dad was going to do to this boy, or pride that his dad was finally doing something good for him, standing up for him.

"Right, hit him."

Nick looked up at his dad.

"What?"

"I said fucking hit him." Nick looked at Steven, who now looked more confused than anything. "Don't just stand there staring at him, fucking hit him."

"I don't want to."

"Why not? This prick's the one who beat you up, isn't he?" Nick nodded again. "So. Hit him. Now." Nick knew there was no getting out of it. He had to do what his dad said, whether he wanted to or not. He took a step towards Steven, whose bravado had returned, and who seemed to have grown to seven foot in the last thirty seconds. Nick balled his fist. He looked back again at his dad, who didn't even say anything this time. Nick swung his arm at Steven, connecting clumsily with the top of his chest. The punch bounced off him harmlessly.

"What the fuck was that?" his dad asked. "Hit him again, properly this time."

Nick swung again, this time connecting with Steven's face, but so weak was the punch that it was barely a tap. This time, Steven swung back, punching Nick painfully in the side of the head. Nick turned back to his dad, waiting for him to intervene. Steven did the same again, but John did nothing. He just stared at his son. Steven hit him again, on the back of the head this time. Nick tried to hit back but Steven had already taken aim with a third punch which he landed right on Nick's nose. Nick looked at his dad again, hoping he'd seen enough now and would stop the fight, but John simply shook his head.

"I don't know why I fucking bother," he said, and turned and walked away. Steven rained a few more blows

140

down on Nick's head and face, a few shouts of "dickhead" and "faggot" joining them. For the next year of primary school after that day, Steven Dunne made it his business to beat Nick on a daily basis, and did so at any other time their paths crossed after Steven had moved up to secondary school.

Now Nick sat, glaring at the back of Steven Dunne's head as he sat and played happy family just metres away from him. For eighteen months or so he'd made his life hell, and it was only the fact that they went to different secondary schools that meant it didn't continue for longer than that. He gripped his coffee mug so hard he thought it would shatter. He placed it down on the table and walked over to their booth.

"Hello, Steven," Nick said, standing over him.

"Alright, Nick," he answered, a little nervously.

"Been a long time, hasn't it, Steven?"

"Yeah, it has, a long time." Steven was shifting uncomfortably in his seat now. "That was all a very long time ago, Nick."

"Not all that long, really, mate." Nick turned and smiled at Steven's wife, who had intuitively picked up on the atmosphere and was looking on warily. The kids seemed oblivious as they competed over an iPad. "Seems quite recent to me. Aren't you gonna introduce me?"

"Karen, this is Nick, we were at school together."

"That we were," Nick said, addressing Karen now. "Were you aware of what a vicious, bullying fuck your husband was?"

"Now, come on," Steven said, his voice attracting the attention of his kids, "let's not do this, not here, not in front of my family, please."

Steven's kids were now watching nervously along with their mother.

"Not in front of your family? I don't remember you being too fucking precious about doing things in front of family when the shoe was on the other foot."

"Look, we were kids. It was three decades ago. I'm a very different person now."

"Yeah, well so am I."

Before Steven had time to respond, Nick picked up the glass ketchup bottle off the table and smashed it into his face. The kids and wife screamed as Nick grabbed him by the throat and punched him in the face, knocking him to the floor. He straddled his chest and punched him again and again. Cries of "Daddy" and "Steven" as well as screams from the few other patrons of the café were the only things drowning out the sound of punch after punch. Nick continued to punch, not sure which parts of the mess he was seeing on Steven's face were blood and which parts were ketchup. He stopped punching and leaned into his ear.

"If you report this, I'll find where you live and I'll fucking kill you. And I'll make your fucking family watch. Then I'll fucking do your happy little family too. I'll cut all their fucking throats, you fucking bullying cunt. Nod if you understand."

Steven nodded his head weakly and Nick wiped his bloody hand on Steven's shirt before getting up. He walked back to his booth and placed some money on the table and walked past Dunne, his wife and kids now gathered around him along with members of staff, and out of the café.

"Oh I'll break them down, no mercy shown.
Heaven knows, it's got to be this time."

PART THREE: MONSTERS

TWENTY-SIX

He stared at the mirror, naked before it. He had crossed the line, and he knew that different rules now applied. He had taken that huge step, now the rules of the rest of society no longer applied to him. He was free. Free from the constraints, the rules that governed everybody else's lives. His friends, the people he worked with, the people that came in and out of his clubs, his family, strangers he passed on the street – they were all subject to the laws, standards, commandments. He pitied them. He laughed out loud at the thought of all the pathetic pieces of shit out there going about their everyday lives; repressed, afraid. He felt no fear now. He had been living in fear, he realised that now. But no more. When the time had come, he hadn't flinched. He hadn't gone into that club planning to do what he did. But in the moment, he had let his true nature take control. The beast within had taken over, and Scott liked it. He didn't feel accountable for what the beast had done. He was two separate beings now. Looking at himself, his perfect form in the mirror, the realisation came to him. There was Scott Collins; a man who went to the gym, went to work, spoke to people, was one of the lads, who did the normal things that people like him did. He was popular, well-liked, desired, respected maybe.

And then, now, there was The Beast. He was a specimen of perfection, driven by his own desires. He did whatever the fuck he wanted. He had lived inside Scott for a long time, and he had been fighting to come out for a long time, but Scott had kept him hidden from the world. Hidden from himself, even. Carrie had helped to keep The Beast tamed. But with her gone, there was nothing to keep him buried, and, as of two nights ago, he had broken free. He had pulled back Scott's flesh to reveal himself. He had ripped his way through Scott's insides, gnawed his way through his bones and organs until he had reached the surface. And when he had reached the surface, there was no stopping him. He was a beautiful, powerful monster, and The Boy had existed only to fulfil the needs of The Beast. And The Beast had devoured him, eaten him whole. He didn't matter, he was nothing, just a fucking piece of meat. He didn't deserve to exist, didn't deserve to breathe the same air as The Beast. Nobody did. Nothing did. Anyone that crossed The Beast's path now was just fuel, fuel for the journey he was on.

TWENTY-SEVEN

"Come on, it'll be fine."

She smiled at him as she spoke, and took his hand in hers. He smiled nervously back at her and squeezed her hand tight.

"That's what you think," he said. He tried to say it as a joke, but he was far from kidding. He put his key in the door and led her inside the house.

"Dad, are you in?"

"In 'ere," his dad shouted from the living room.

Nick's heart jumped. He knew that tone of voice. His dad's voice took on a scratchy, raspy quality when he had been drinking. And although it was barely midday, Nick knew instantly just how drunk his dad was. He hesitated, frozen to the spot in the hallway. He thought about dragging Julie out of the house and running down the street and away from this house, away from him.

"You comin' in then or what?"

"Go on," Julie whispered.

Nick opened the door of the living room and stepped inside. John was sitting in his chair in the corner of the room, cans scattered around his feet, a bottle of whiskey in one hand being tipped into the tumbler in the other.

"Dad?"

"Hmm?"

"Dad, I've got someone I'd like you to meet."

"Not the fucking Queen, is it? If it is, you can tell that fat, old slag to do one, heh-he-heh."

"No, it's someone from college."

"Oh aye? Hope it's not some hippy lecturer."

"No, she's a student too."

"She? A girl, eh? Fucking hell, you should have said.

Bring her in, then."

He stood up and put his drink down on the floor next to his chair. He quickly tucked his shirt in and checked his hair in the mirror. Nick came back into the room with a pretty young girl.

"Dad, this is Julie."

John rubbed his hand against the leg of his jeans and extended it out to Julie.

"Nice to meet you, Julie."

"Nice to meet you too, Mr Hanman."

"I don't know a Mr Hanman. My name's John, so that's what you call me, darling. Right?"

"OK, Mr Han— sorry – John."

"There, that's more like it. Much more friendly. Isn't it, Nick?"

Nick nodded. He looked at his dad's hand, Julie's hand still held tightly in it. He gestured towards the couch.

"Have a seat, love," he said, and sat down on the couch next to her. As Julie sat down her skirt rode up above her knees. Only for a moment, but long enough for John to notice. Nick knew full well he would have noticed.

"So, how did you and our Nicky meet, then?"

"Well, we're in the same class at college."

"Oh, yeah, course you are. So, he chatted you up, then, did he?"

"Dad..."

"Dad what? I'm talking to Julie, not you. Go on, Julie, love. You were telling me how my son managed to get his dirty little paws on you."

Julie laughed nervously.

"Don't mind me, Julie. I'm just messing with you. That's just my sense of humour, isn't it, Nicky?"

Nick nodded his head.

"I said isn't it, Nicky?"

"Y-yes, Dad."

"Speak up!"

"Yes, Dad."

"Quiet as a fucking mouse, this one, isn't he, Julie?"

148

Again, she laughed awkwardly.

"That's a lovely laugh you've got, Julie."

He edged closer to her along the couch.

"Sorry, Julie, where are my manners? Can I get you a drink, love?"

"No, thanks, I don't really drink."

"Oh, come on, it's a bit of a special occasion, isn't it? Let's see what I've got."

He leaned over to his side of the couch and rummaged in the plastic bag beside it.

"Well, you don't strike me as a beer or whiskey drinker."

Another nervous laugh.

"Dad, it's alright, we're going to meet some friends soon, anyway."

"You've got time for a drink with your dad. Haven't you, Julie?"

This time she remained silent.

"Tell you what, Nick," John continued, reaching for his wallet and pulling out some notes, "why don't you pop down to the shops and get us something to drink? Maybe get some vodka and a bottle of Coke for Julie."

Nick's eyes met Julie's and she made an imploring face at him, telling him not to leave her alone here.

"It's alright, Dad, we'd best get going."

"I told you, you've got time for a drink with your dad."

Again he met Julie's imploring eyes.

"No, it's—"

John cut him off with a slap to the face.

"What?"

"I was saying—"

This time a back-hander across the face stopped him. Nick put his hand to his lip and wiped away the trickle of blood there.

"What?"

"Nothing."

"That's better. Now go on, off you fuck to the shop.

And don't rush. Me and Julie are gonna get acquainted, aren't we, Julie?"

Nick looked briefly at Julie, who was almost in tears now, but his dad grabbed the back of his neck and turned his head away from her, simultaneously pushing him towards the door.

"Nick."

John pushed Nick further away from the pleading voice of his girlfriend.

"Nick?"

Nick headed down the hallway to the front door and opened it, hearing his voice called behind him one last time before he closed it.

"Nick? Nick!"

Nick lifted his head up from the desk. He wiped away the slobber that had crusted at the corner of his mouth. Unsure of where he was, he sat up when he saw Kathleen leaning close into him. He knocked the empty whiskey bottle onto the floor, where it made a dull thud as it bounced on the thick carpet.

"Nick? What the hell are you doing here?"

"What? Oh, I just, erm, I worked late, must have just dozed off."

"Dozed off, eh? Well, drinking an entire bottle of whiskey will do that to you."

Nick ignored her and stood up unsteadily from his desk, trying to rub the fug from his face. He walked to the small fridge he kept in the corner of the office and took a bottle of water from it. He ripped the top off and drank with the vigour only a man with a severe hangover can muster. He walked back to his desk and took some paracetamols from the drawer and knocked them back, washing them down with the rest of the water. He keenly avoided Kathleen's eyes, which he felt on him the whole time.

"What's going on, Nick?"

He finally turned to face her.

"What do you mean? Nothing's going on."

"Nothing's going on? Nick, you're drinking again, for

150

a start. And you slept here. On your desk. You've got a couch right there." She gestured to the couch in the corner of the room. "You couldn't even make it to the opposite side of the room. Even when you're drinking or doing... whatever else it is you do, you usually manage to make it home. I've worked for you for long enough to know when something's wrong, Nick, even without those obvious warning signs, so please don't lie to me. What's happened?"

Nick walked over to the neglected couch and collapsed into it, his head hanging right back.

"Lisa's kicked me out. Two nights ago."

"Well that much I've ascertained. Why?"

Nick shook his head.

"Fucking hell. Where to begin? The drinking."

"Drugs?"

He nodded his head.

"The long hours, the secrecy, the... everything."

"OK, but you've got past this stuff before, haven't you?" Kathleen said, joining him on the couch.

"It's different this time."

"Why?"

"I... there was... I crashed the car. With Monica in it."

"Oh my God, Nick. Is she—"

"She's fine. It wasn't a bad one, just a dink really. She wasn't hurt, just shaken up."

"I bet she was. What happened? You weren't drunk, were you?"

Nick shook his head.

"I'd done some coke."

"Oh, for Christ's sake, Nick. What the hell were you thinking?"

"Don't, Kathleen. You don't need to say anything, I know how badly I've fucked up. Trust me, there's absolutely nothing you can say to me I haven't already thought myself a thousand times."

"Alright, fair enough. So what are you going to do about it? How do you plan to put it right?"

"Put it right? Are you fucking kidding me? There's no

putting this right. That's it. I'm fucked. There's no getting past this. There's no reconciliation, no working it out."

"So you're just going to give up?"

"It's not a case of giving up. It's a case of having completely fucked something beyond all repair."

"But you can't just – "

She turned away from him.

"I can't just what?"

"I'm sorry, maybe I'm speaking out of turn. I realise I'm just someone who works for you."

"Come on, Kathleen, you know you're much more to me than that. You can say what you want to me, but it won't change anything."

"Nick, it's been two nights."

"Yeah?"

"It's been two nights and you're drinking yourself unconscious at your desk. If you don't fix this somehow, then what are you going to be doing in two months' time? In two years' time?"

"What the fuck do you want me to do, Kathleen? She's finally had enough of my shit, and I don't fucking blame her. I'm fucking poisonous. Her and Monica are better off without me."

"That's not true, Nick. Monica adores you. I've seen how she is with you, and how you are around her. She needs her daddy."

Nick put his face in his palms and began to cry.

"And what about Lisa?"

"Well, she's stuck with you until now, she needs you too, Nick. She just needs you to... be a better Nick than you're being right now. You can't just give up. I know it's easy for me to say but you have to try. Trust me; if you do nothing then you'll look back in a few years with so much regret. You have to be able to at least tell yourself that you tried. That you did everything you could."

Nick nodded his head and stood up from the couch, rubbing his face.

"You're right. I need to get my shit together. I'm

going over there now."

"No, Nick. Not yet."

"What do you mean? You've just spent the last five minutes convincing me to try."

"Look at yourself, Nick. You look like shit, you stink of booze. Get over to the club, get yourself a sauna, have a shave and put a clean suit on."

"Yeah. Yeah, yeah, of course. What the fuck am I thinking? I can't go and see her looking like this. Thanks, Kath, you're a fucking star."

Nick grabbed his car keys from the desk and headed out the door.

*

The Primavera Health Club, located in a leafy part of Formby. Membership fees of over a hundred pounds a month, with some of the best facilities on Merseyside. Nick had been a member for years, and often brought clients and potential clients here. Apart from for schmoozing purposes, he rarely used the facilities himself, but today they were most welcome. Alone in the sauna, he closed his eyes and leant back against the hard marble. He felt the booze sweating its way out of his system. He felt himself drifting off, deciding that there was no point rushing to see Lisa, that a snooze could only help.

As soon as he was asleep, though, he saw Francis's face, twisted in pain, blue/purple tongue sticking obscenely out between his teeth. Then Nick was standing in a morgue, Francis naked on a slab in front of him. A man without a face handed Nick a scalpel and gestured for him to begin. Nick hesitantly inserted the scalpel below Francis's sternum and cut downwards to his pubis. He put the blade down, took a hold of either side of his incision and pulled the abdomen apart. He felt the layers of fat and tissue tearing as he pulled, until it was wide open. He turned to the faceless man, who had moved to the corner of the room. He slowly nodded his head. Nick leant over Francis and peered inside his abdomen. Inside, a small foetus, about the size of Nick's fist, was writhing. Nick felt vomit rising inside him; a deep breath pushed it down. He looked back to the faceless man, who made no gesture. He

153

heard a small, ripping sound and looked back to Francis. The foetus had poked its hand through the flesh that surrounded it and was trying to pull itself out. Nick panicked and tried to close the abdomen back over but, quicker than he was able to do so, the foetus was pushing its way out. Nick folded the flaps of skin down and tried to push them together but a tiny hand reached out and over, starting to push the flaps back. Nick backed away, unsure what to do; he turned and tried to run but tripped, slamming his face into the tiled floor.

He woke up with a yelp in the sauna, slumped on his side. He looked up and saw there were now two other men in there with him. One of them was openly staring at him, the other trying to pretend he wasn't watching him out of the corner of his eye. Nick realised he'd pissed himself. He got up and headed for the showers.

He stood at the sink, shaving. Long, slow, deliberate strokes of the blade across his face, across his throat. He rinsed the razor under the tap and poured some aftershave into his palms. He massaged it into his neck and slapped it onto his face, drumming his hands against his cheeks. He took a deep breath. He slapped himself hard against the side of his face. He slapped the other side. Then the other. Then the other. He slapped himself back and forth, harder each time, till there were red welts on both cheeks. He leaned into the mirror.

"Don't fuck this up," he growled to his reflection. "Don't you fucking make a mess of this. This is your last fucking chance now, *don't you fucking dare mess this up, you useless fucking cunt.*"

He slapped himself one last time. In the mirror, he noticed the man who had been watching him in the sauna now standing at the urinal, watching him.

"Fuck you looking at, pal?"

The man looked away.

At his locker, he took the fresh suit out of the dry cleaner's bag and slipped it on. He was fixing his tie when he heard his phone vibrate on the bench. He reached for it without hesitation and looked at the screen. It was Epson. His thumb hovered over the "answer" button, but he didn't take

154

the call. The "missed call" message appeared on the screen. Instantly, Michael's name reappeared on the caller display. He put the phone down and finished with his tie. Seconds later his phone went again, this time the text alert. He looked at the phone. One voicemail from Michael Epson. He slipped the phone into his pocket, slammed the locker door shut and headed for his car.

*

He pulled onto the driveway and was relieved to see Lisa's car there. He had half expected her to have gone to her mum's. He hesitated at the front door, actually considered knocking for a second before realising how ridiculous it would be. He entered the house, anticipating the sound of Monica charging towards him, and was crushed when it didn't materialise. He walked towards the kitchen, not a sound coming from anywhere in the house. Lisa was sat at the breakfast bar, sipping from a cup of coffee.

"What are you doing here?" she asked without looking at him.

Nick walked over to the counter and poured himself a coffee.

"I came to talk."

"There's nothing to say."

"There's a lot to say."

"No, Nick. There isn't. I've said everything I've got to say to you. That's it. It's over."

Nick placed his cup down on the breakfast bar but didn't take a seat.

"Lisa, please. Don't do this."

"It's you that's done this, Nick, not me. Don't even try to—"

"I'm not, I'm not trying to blame you. I'm really not. I know it's down to me. Everything that's happened, everything that's gone wrong, it's all down to me."

Lisa put her face in her hands; her shoulders began lightly convulsing.

"You know what, Nick? It actually isn't all just down to you. It's me too. I've let you get away with so much for so long. All the drinking, all the drugs, all the secrecy. I've let it slide because I wanted all this."

"All what?"

"Everything," she screamed, turning to face him for the first time. "The money, the clothes, the cars, this fucking house." She picked her cup up and launched it across the room, where it shattered against the tiled floor. "I told myself for a while that it wasn't for me. I told myself that I was doing what was right for Monica. That I was just giving her the best possible start. I convinced myself it was for her. And I exposed her. I exposed her to a father who's never here. Who's drunk and high half the time when he is. Who fills the house with... with anger, with confusion, with... darkness. For years, I exposed her to all that. God knows what emotional damage it's done to her already, being around all that. And now, if that wasn't enough, you crash the car with her in it. For the first time, she's actually been put in physical danger. She could have been killed, all because of my greed and your... your fucking addictions. I don't know which of us is worse."

"I'm worse, Lisa," he said, now taking a seat. "You're a wonderful mum, it's me that's the fuck-up. You've always tried to do your best, but I've always held you back." He reached across the breakfast bar and tried to take her hand, but she pulled it away. "Please, Lisa, I'm asking you for one more chance. I swear to you, this has been the wake-up call I've needed."

"So every other time I've kicked you out, made you go to rehab, given you ultimatums, what were they? What I say means fuck all to you?"

"No of course not, it's just... it was Monica, like you said. I've never put her in harm's way before."

This time Lisa shut him up by actually laughing at him.

"Never put her in harm's way? I never said that, Nick. All I said was that you'd never put her in physical danger before. She's been in harm's way from the day she was born. Emotional harm. And we've both put her there."

"So what are you saying? Where does that leave us? Leave me?"

Lisa shook her head and got down from the stool. She walked to the cupboard and took out a dustpan and brush. She knelt down and swept up the coffee mug she'd broken.

"I don't know, Nick. What I know is that I'll no longer put myself first. From now on it's all about Monica and what's best for her. And I'm sorry to say, but I haven't yet figured out what part you'll have to play in that, if any. So, for now, at least, you need to leave while I try and figure that out."

She hadn't even finished speaking and he was down off his stool, out of the kitchen and out the front door. He sped out of the driveway and back towards town. He felt his phone vibrating in his pocket. He took it out and looked at the caller display. Epson again. He pulled over to the side of the road. Nick slammed his fist against the steering wheel three times, the beeps this produced attracting the attention of a passing old man, who stopped and peered in through the passenger side window.

"FUCK OFF!" Nick snarled when he noticed him. He pulled blindly back into traffic, causing a few cars to slam on their brakes as he did so.

He pulled into the car park of his building and into his space. He turned the engine off and sat back in his seat. He turned the mirror towards himself. He took some deep breaths, trying to control the urge to cry.

"Don't you fucking dare," he said to his reflection. "Don't you dare cry, you fucking little baby."

He slapped himself hard.

"Get a fucking grip. Get your fucking shit together and get up there."

He opened his glove box and took out the flask. He unscrewed the lid, held it to his nose and took a deep breath in. He put it to his lips and began to tilt it, but stopped just before it touched his lips. He screwed the lid back on and threw it back in the glove box. He slammed the glove box shut and put his hand on the door handle. His hand rested there for a moment, then moved back to the glove box, taking out the flask again. He took the lid off again, held the flask tightly in his hand for what could have been half a minute or half an hour. He took one more look at his reflection and put the flask back and got out of the car.

He headed to the lift and pushed the button for the top floor. He considered stopping it on his floor but decided to keep going. He stepped out onto the top floor and walked to the reception desk. The receptionist looked up from her typing.

"Afternoon, Nick, he's expecting you, he said to send you straight through."

Of course he was expecting him. It didn't matter how many of Michael's phone calls Nick ignored. It was inevitable he'd go back to him sooner rather than later. Nick walked up to the door and turned the handle, braced himself and plastered on a look of defiance and pushed the door open. Epson was sat behind his desk, already watching the door, as though he could sense Nick approaching.

"Nick. It's good to see you. Come in and sit down."

Nick attempted to walk with defiance and cockiness, but he felt his legs shaking as he approached. He looked down at the floor, but could feel Michael's eyes burrowing into the top of his head. He thought he wouldn't even reach the chair before his legs gave out, but just about managed to do so, collapsing into it but trying to disguise it as a deliberate drop.

Nick kept his eyes on the ground, waiting for Michael to speak. For what felt like hours, he waited for Michael to speak. Eventually, Nick cracked, looking meekly up at him.

"I'm sorry I missed your calls earlier. I was... in the middle of something."

Still Michael said nothing, instead nodding along like a GP who's only half paying attention, but his eyes burning deep into Nick. Reading him.

"I, erm... had to go and see Lisa."

"'Go' and see her? But you live together, Nick."

"Well, not at this precise moment, we don't."

Michael leant back in his chair and nodded slowly.

"I see. I'm not surprised. When you didn't answer my calls I thought it must be either family-related or related to your... fondness for indulgence, shall we say? Though I suspect it is probably a combination of both factors."

"Well, I'd rather not go into it, to be honest."

"Really?" Michael said, his tone changing in an instant, his demeanour changing from that of a concerned elder to a controlling adversary just as quickly. "Well, if that's how you feel, Nick, far be it from me to pry into your private affairs." He walked over to his drinks cabinet and returned with a thick glass tumbler and a bottle of Hennessy brandy. He stared Nick out as he unscrewed the bottle top and poured himself a small measure. He knocked it back in one, still staring Nick out, then poured himself a larger one, and sat back in his chair.

"You'll excuse me not offering you a drink, Nick, but I think under the current circumstances it might not be wise of you to partake. Oh, I'm sorry. Does that constitute meddling in your personal affairs?"

Nick looked away. He turned his head to the bookshelves that covered almost an entire wall of the huge office. At the centre of it, a framed photo of Michael with his wife and children.

"I asked you a question, Nick."

"No."

"I'm sorry? No, what?"

"No, it wouldn't be... wise."

"What wouldn't be wise, Nick?" Michael asked as he took a sip from the tumbler.

"For me to... partake."

"And what else?"

Nick stared at the photo. The embodiment of family happiness. Togetherness.

"No, it wouldn't be meddling."

"Well, what a relief. You see, I thought I must have somehow caused you great offence. I mean, a whole day's worth of missed calls. Ignored calls, presumably. I could only conclude you were harbouring some sort of deep anger towards me. Was I wrong to think that, Nick?"

"I... I just had to do some thinking. Just had to get my head right."

"Some thinking? Get your head right? Might I make a suggestion?"

Nick nodded, knowing he wasn't really being asked for permission.

"You are, and always have been, at your best when you're focussed on your work. Whether your home life has been stable or turbulent, whether your inner demons have been under control or rampant, you have never been better than when you give your work your full energy and attention. Now, of course, I'm not saying you should neglect your family. Of course I'm not saying that. But you need to remember how to, shall we say, compartmentalise."

Nick almost laughed at that word. Compartmentalise. How many times had he told Lisa, told himself, that he could "compartmentalise"?

"Take comfort in your work," Michael continued. "Let it drive you. Take whatever negative feelings or energy you're currently experiencing and channel them into work. Trust me, you'll feel better for it. And I suspect your home life will benefit. I feel sure of that, Nick. And if things at home are beyond repair, then it will simply free up more of your time to do what you do best."

Nick felt his fist clenching. He wanted to pick up the tumbler and shove it into Michael's face. He wanted to smash the bottle over his head and use the jagged edges to rip out his throat. But most of all, he just wanted to taste the brandy that was just inches away from him.

"Alright, let me put it another way. The next time you drive up to that big, beautiful house of yours in your expensive car, and see the wonderful clothes your wife and daughter are wearing, remember where all that comes from. Remember what I've done for you, Nick. And remember, even if the worst comes to the worst on the home front, the very least you will be able to do is to look after them – financially, at least. You'll always have that, even if nothing else, to offer them.

And the reason you will always be able to do that is talking to you right now."

Nick stood up quickly, the chair falling to the ground behind him. Michael flinched only slightly.

"I hate having to talk to you this way, Nick. But it seems to me you're in need of a clarification session."

"What do you mean?"

Michael stood up from his desk.

"I mean, you're forgetting one very simple rule that we have. And that is, that no matter what is happening, no matter what is going on, YOU DO NOT IGNORE MY FUCKING PHONE CALLS, NICK!"

This time it was Nick who flinched. He took a step back from Michael. Nick sometimes forgot how physically imposing Michael was. Tall, broad-shouldered, and he'd kept himself in good shape over the years. But Nick knew that if it came to a straight fight, Michael wouldn't stand a chance against him.

"Now do we understand each other, Nick?"

Nick turned to look at the photo again. He remembered the face of the boy in the hotel room all those years ago. He thought of the teenager he'd personally delivered to the hotel just a few nights ago.

"I said, do we understand each other?"

Nick thought of the dozens of young boys he'd facilitated over the years. What might have become of them since. If they were damaged like he was, and what part he'd had to play in that. He turned around and headed for the door.

"Nick? Where the hell do you think you're going?"

He didn't look back, he opened the door.

"Nick, I'm talking to you. Nick!"

He slammed the door shut.

TWENTY-EIGHT

"Fucking faggot. Fucking dirty little queer."

Scott grabbed the back of the man's head and shoved his face down into the pillow.

"Fucking bastard. Fucking slut."

He slammed his cock into the man's arse as hard as he could, taking the full length out before ramming it balls-deep back in.

"You love that big fucking cock up your arse, don't you, faggot?"

"Mm-hmm," the man mumbled unconvincingly.

"I said you love it, don't you, faggot?"

"Yes, I love it," he said, with more effort this time.

"Fucking say it, then."

"What?"

"I said, fucking say it."

"Say what?"

"That you love that big fucking cock up your arse."

"I love that big fucking cock up my arse."

"Again. Keep saying it."

"I love that big fucking cock up my arse. I love that big fucking cock up my arse."

"Louder."

"Oh, I just LOVE that big fucking cock up my arse. Oh, it feels SO good, Daddy."

Scott stopped pounding.

"You taking the fucking piss?"

"No, of course not."

"Well it fucking sounds like it."

Then he sighed. The faggot actually fucking *sighed*. Scott considered reaching down and wrapping his hands round either side of his jaw, wrenching his head back and snapping

162

his little faggoty neck.

"Come on, let's just get this over with, you've only got another five minutes left anyway."

Scott thought about just chocking him to death then and there. But he decided to get his money's worth.

"Alright, if that's how you wanna be. Let's get this over with."

Scott pulled his cock out and whipped the condom off and rammed his cock back in. He started pounding him as hard as he had before, but now he built up the pace. He fucked him as hard as he could, as fast as he could. The faggot kept his mouth shut but Scott could hear him wincing with every thrust. He punched him in the back of the head.

"Ow! What the fuck?"

"Yeah, not so fucking sarcastic now, are you, faggot?"

"No fucking rough stuff!"

"Rough? This isn't rough," Scott said as he slapped him on the side of the face. "Nor's this," he said as he slapped the other side.

"Enough."

"This might be a bit rough, though."

He grabbed his throat and squeezed hard. He made wheezing noises as Scott pounded away, feeling his balls contract until he exploded inside him. He released his grip on his throat as he came, just before the faggot passed out.

Scott pulled out and rolled away. He sat on the edge of the bed and looked at his reflection in the hotel room mirror.

The faggot ran to the bathroom. He didn't shut the door and Scott could see him examining his throat for marks or damage. He came back into the bedroom and looked over at Scott. Scott glared at him, giving him that look he knew could scare the shit out of people. The faggot looked away.

"That's gonna cost you extra," he said quietly as he began to get dressed.

"What is?"

"That. All that shit you pulled. We never discussed anything like that."

Scott shrugged.

"I mean it."

Scott stood up and took a step towards him.

"Do you?"

He hesitated.

"Yeah. I mean it."

"You'll get what we agreed, not a fucking penny more, faggot."

"No way. You need to pay more. An extra twenty."

Scott picked up his jeans and took his wallet out.

"Come and take it then, faggot."

He stared at Scott's wallet but didn't move.

"Come on. If you want it so much, come and take it. Faggot. Queer."

"Fuck you. Fucking keep it. Fucking closet case."

"You fucking what?"

"I said you're a closet case," he said, turning away and putting his jacket on. "Not my fault if you can't admit what you are. And that makes you more of a faggot than me."

"What did you call me?"

The faggot turned to face him.

"I said you're a fucking closet-queer faggot!"

Scott punched him as hard as he could across the face. Following instantly through with another. He fell to the ground and Scott kicked him in the face, and again in the ribs. As he struggled to his knees, Scott grabbed his hair, lifting his head up. He punched him in the face again and again until he went limp in his grip. Scott dropped him to the floor and watched with amusement as he made a pathetic attempt to crawl towards the door. Scott looked down at his still-naked body and realised he was hard again. He reached down and grabbed him by his collar and dragged him towards the bed. He dropped him so his top half was on the bed, kneeling on the floor. Scott pulled his jeans down and entered him again.

TWENTY-NINE

More dreams. This time Nick was his dad, and he was talking down to Nick, but Nick was Francis. Francis kept reaching up to him, but Nick kept smacking his hands away. Nick, but Nick as his dad. He couldn't quite get his head round it. Even within the dream, it didn't make any sense. In the end, he poured a bottle of whiskey all over Francis and set him on fire. But instead of running around or screaming, Francis just went and sat in the chair in the corner. Nick sat in the chair opposite and watched him burn.

Nick woke up and rolled straight off the bed. He scrambled to the bathroom and vomited into the toilet, then collapsed onto the floor and leant against the bathroom wall, panting for breath. He crawled to the sink and pulled himself slowly up. He reached out to the taps with shaking hands and turned them on, and splashed his face with cold water and attempted to cup his hand to bring some water up to his mouth, but his hand was shaking so much he couldn't do it. Nick left the tap running and staggered back to the bedroom and picked up the bottle of whiskey from the bedside table. He unscrewed the lid and swigged the last few mouthfuls and collapsed back onto the bed, where he turned onto his side, facing the same table he'd taken the whiskey from. He snorted a line and lay on his back. Nick looked at his wrist and saw his watch was missing. He picked up the clock on the opposite bedside table. It was close to three in the afternoon. He wanted to go back to sleep but didn't want to face any more of the dreams. He reached for the remote and switched the TV on. He flicked through a few channels before stopping on the local news. He leaned back over to do another line, only half listening to the news.

"...a body found in woods two days ago has been identified as that of eighteen-year-old Christian McGann."

The name registered with Nick but he wasn't sure where from. He put his folded note back down to do another line.

"...*he had been severely beaten and strangled. Police are appealing for information.*"

He looked up from his coke and turned to the TV and nearly vomited again when he saw him. The boy. He only glimpsed his face for a split second but it was long enough. He knew instantly. He picked the remote up again and flicked frantically through the channels, looking for more local news, but found nothing. He picked up his phone and logged into the hotel's broadband and searched local news, Twitter feeds and websites. Nothing but vague references. "*Local teen named in murder enquiry*". "*Teen murder victim named*".

He logged into Facebook and typed in "Christian McGann Liverpool". Dozens of results came up. He scrolled down the thumbnail profile pictures till he saw him. He clicked on the profile and saw the reams of posts on the wall.

R.I.P. mate
Life won't be the same without you
Can't believe you're gone
Hope they catch the bastard

The teary emoticons, the memes with the trite quotes about death and loss, the pictures of him with his friends.

This time he couldn't hold back the vomit. He ran back to the bathroom and made it to the sink before he threw up. Even when he was empty, his guts contracted and forced out more fluid until he was just retching and heaving over the sink, a thick layer of spittle hanging from his bottom lip. He walked back to the bedroom and paced the floor.

"Epson, Epson, Epson. Fucking Epson," he muttered to himself. "What the fuck have you done? What the fuck have you done?"

He picked up the empty whiskey bottle and smashed it against the far wall.

"What the fuck? What the fuck? What-the-fuck-what-the-fuck-what-the-fuck?"

He picked up his phone again. Maybe he'd made a

mistake. He'd been drinking all night. Perhaps he'd got it all horribly wrong. He checked the Facebook profile again. There must be a hundred Christian McGanns in Liverpool. Probably half a dozen that looked like that. He clicked on the photo albums and his heart sank. It was no mistake. He clicked on picture after picture. That face was unmistakable. Those features, that hair. There was no doubt. It was that same boy. That same boy he'd driven to this very same hotel.

A knock at the door.

"Fuck off!"

Another knock.

"Mr Hanman? Is everything alright in there?"

Nick walked over to the door and opened it a crack. The guy from reception took a step back. One of the security guys was hovering behind his right shoulder.

"What do you want?"

"Is everything OK in there, Mr Hanman? Some other guests have complained about the noise. A sound of something breaking?" The security gorilla arched his neck, trying to see past Nick into the room.

"Oh yeah, I just... dropped a glass."

The receptionist nodded slowly.

"Right. Is everything else alright?"

Nick looked from the receptionist to the security guy.

"You were on the night I brought him here," he said to the security guy.

"I'm sorry?"

"Probably some of the others too."

"Mr Hanman, I'm afraid if you can't keep the noise down I'm going to have to ask—"

"Don't worry," Nick cut him off, "I'm checking out in a minute anyway."

He closed the door. He opened up the spy hole in the door and watched as the two unwelcome visitors hesitated, then shrugged their shoulders and walked away. He walked back into the room and dressed quickly, gathering up the few belongings he'd brought with him. Before he left he clogged up the plug holes of the sink and bath and turned the taps on full. He pulled the TV off the wall and turned the mattress over onto the floor before taking the lift down to reception. He threw the key onto the counter and walked out to the car park, got into the car and turned on the engine, and just sat there, staring dead ahead for a while. He checked the time. Twenty-past-three in the afternoon. He thought for a minute what day it must be. He was pretty sure it was Thursday. He thought for another second, then screeched out of the car park.

*

The girl on the front desk looked up as the lift pinged, the usual insincere grin plastered on her face. The grin disappeared as she got a look at Nick, his unkempt appearance, no tie, shirt unbuttoned at the neck and hanging out of his trousers, a few days' worth of stubble.

"Is he in?" Nick asked, barely slowing down as he passed the desk.

"Yes, but you can't go in there, Nick, he's got someone in there with him. Nick."

Her voice faded as Nick stormed towards Epson's office and opened the door. He was sat behind his desk, leaning back in his chair. Another guy Nick vaguely recognised was sitting opposite him. They both turned to face Nick as he entered.

"Nick? What do you think you're doing? I'm in a meeting."

"Yeah, with me."

The other guy's eyes darted back and forth from Nick to Epson.

"Wait outside, Nick. I'm busy."

Epson turned away, back to the other guy.

"What were you saying, James?"

"Erm, yes, so the report is generally very positive – "

"Remember, Michael, you called me in to talk about that murdered lad. That friend of yours."

James stopped and stared at Epson, then turned his head slightly to look at Nick. Epson cocked his head slightly at Nick, eyes narrowing slightly in curiosity.

"Actually, James, I do need to speak to Nick here

168

about something. We'll finish this up later."

James gathered up some papers he'd had on the desk and scurried out, glancing at Nick as he left.

"What the hell is wrong with you, Nick?" Epson asked calmly as the door closed.

"What the fuck did you do, Michael?"

"What do you mean?"

"Don't fucking play games with me, Michael! I know what you fucking did!"

Epson leaned back further in his chair.

"I have no idea what you're blathering about, Nick. But you'd better start making sense very quickly, because I have neither the time nor the patience for this."

"You fucking killed him. Didn't you? Or had someone do it for you?"

Epson stood up from his desk and walked slowly over to the drinks cabinet.

"I'm loath to offer you a drink, Nick. Judging by your appearance and the smell coming from you, you've had plenty already," he said, pouring a large brandy. He walked over to Nick and held it out. "But I think you'd better drink this, calm down and tell me what the hell you're going on about."

Nick smacked the drink from his hand, sending it flying across the room, making a thick thudding sound as it bounced off the carpet.

"I don't want a fucking drink. I wanna know what you fucking did."

Epson took a step back, his demeanour remaining calm, but a flash of caution appearing in his eyes.

"Nick, I assure you, I don't know what you're talking about. Explain yourself."

"The boy. The fucking boy."

"What boy?"

"The one I brought to the hotel for you. A couple of weeks back."

Epson thought for a second and nodded his head almost imperceptibly.

"What about him?"

169

"He's dead. Fucking murdered."

"Murdered?"

"Don't fucking play dumb with me, you cunt. You fucking did it."

"What? Why would I do that?"

"I don't fucking know. Maybe he threatened you. Maybe he said he'd expose you. Like Francis did."

Epson slapped him hard across the face.

"Nick. Get. A fucking. Grip. Think for a moment. Think about what you're saying. How many times have you brought... people to meet me. In those circumstances."

"I don't fucking know..."

"How many, Nick?"

"I DIDN'T FUCKING COUNT, MICHAEL! I don't know, a lot."

"And, to the best of your knowledge, Nick, how many of them have wound up *being fucking murdered*?"

Nick ran his hands through his hair, paced the room.

"How. Many?"

"None. Fucking none."

"That's right, Nick. None. The only associate of ours who ended up that way has already been mentioned during the course of this bizarre and offensive conversation. And to whom did I go? To perform that particular task?"

"Me."

"That's right, Nick. You. So you will perhaps note the irony of you coming over here, barging into my office, accusing me of... whatever it is you're accusing me of, taking the moral fucking high ground with me, after what you've done for me, and after the kind of rewards you've accepted from me for it. I trust the irony of that is not lost on you, Nick?"

Nick leaned back against the wall, breathing deeply. He nodded his head slowly.

"Anyway. Who cares, Nick? He was just some little teen whore who sucked cock and sold his arse for money. It's no wonder he wound up dead. Fuck him."

Nick lashed the back of his hand across Epson's face.

170

Epson put a hand up to where Nick's hand had connected, a look of shock on his face. He pulled his hand away slowly to reveal a gash across his left cheek, with blood running from it. Nick looked at the back of his hand, a thin layer of skin stuck to his wedding ring. Epson looked at the palm of his hand, the ink blot line of blood there. He took a handkerchief from his pocket and pressed it to his face.

"Get out," he said, his face contorted with the kind of anger Nick had never seen him display before.

Nick turned and started walking towards the door. He stopped and turned his head back towards Epson.

"He wasn't just some whore. He was a young man. He was a person. A person who was worth more than ten of you."

"You're finished, Nick. Do you hear me? *Fucking finished.*"

Nick took a few steps towards Michael and enjoyed watching him cower backwards, knocking into his desk. Nick pushed his face right up to his.

"I was finished long before I ever met you."

THIRTY

Scott lifted the barbell off the floor. One more set of fifty reps. An extra twenty kilos for this last go round. He took a step closer to the floor-to-ceiling mirror and began lifting. He reached fifty reps in well under a minute. He decided to keep going. He stepped closer yet to the mirror. The barbell felt almost weightless in his hands, but his biceps burned. He loved that feeling. He leaned his head closer to the mirror, so close his breath and spit landed on it. He grunted louder now with each rep as he felt his arms begin to weaken. A hundred reps. He kept going. He was oblivious to the stares around the gym pointing his way as he grunted louder and louder. One hundred and seventy-five reps. He kept going. He pushed on through the pain that was now shooting up his arms, into his shoulders and neck. Two hundred and fifty reps.

"*Yaaaargh!*" he yelled as he let the weight crash to the floor.

He leaned his face right into the mirror, his forehead touching that of his reflection.

"*Fucking come on! Fucking three hundred.*"

He slammed his palms against the huge mirror, causing it to shake violently. He turned and walked away, leaving two huge, sweaty palm prints fading on the mirror. He looked as other gym users looked at the floor or turned their backs as he approached and walked past them, staring every one of the weak little fuckers down.

Back in the locker room he injected himself with another 50mg of Deca Durabolin and took another Anavar tablet, washed down with a protein shake. He reached into his jeans pocket and pulled out a wrap of coke. He started walking towards the toilet then stopped. Fuck it. Why go to the toilets? He could do whatever the fuck he wanted. Who was going to stop him? If anyone was stupid enough to get in his way, he would simply unleash The Beast on them. He opened up the wrap and knelt in front of the bench. He laid the coke in a line on the bench and snorted a nice, long line of it. He grabbed his bag and drove home in his gym clothes.

When he got home he went straight upstairs and stripped off in front of the full-length mirror in the bedroom. He examined himself from every angle, filming himself on his iPhone as he turned so he could see every possible angle. He flexed his chest muscles in particular. They were looking better than ever, but the layer of hair was covering the definition a little.

He went to the bathroom and turned on the shower and stood at the sink while it warmed up and took the hair clippers from the cabinet before cutting his hair, what little there was of it, as short as the clippers would do, then he did the same with his pubic hair. He picked up his razor and shaving foam and stepped into the shower, where he rubbed the foam over his chest and shaved it. He did the same to the stubble that remained of his pubic hair, then covered his legs in foam and slowly and carefully shaved them. Even his feet and toes. He foamed and shaved his armpits before covering what was left of his hair and shaving it off, looking in the shower mirror. He stepped from the shower and walked back to the bedroom. He stood in front of the mirror and held his arms out at the side of him in a Christ-like pose. He looked at himself. Hairless, muscular, his cock hanging between his legs. Scott stared at it and felt the blood beginning to flow there. He took it in his hand and began to slowly rub it, feeling it getting harder as he did so. He continued until it was full and engorged. He turned to the side and looked at his side profile, muscularity on show, huge cock jutting out in front of him. He began to wank himself off slowly, flexing his muscles as he did so. He looked so fucking good, perfect now. He turned to face himself again as he pumped his cock harder, it feeling hard as granite in his hand. He flexed the bicep of his free arm, wanking harder now, flexing every muscle he could see, until he came all over his reflection.

THIRTY-ONE

Detective Sergeant Paul Jenkins left the station. It was almost midday, and nearly twenty hours since he first went on duty. He hadn't had a full day off in nearly a fortnight, and hadn't had a decent night's sleep in at least as long. He debated whether to go for a full English then home to bed or a quick pub lunch and a couple of pints. As he reached the car, he heard his name being shouted behind him.

"Paul. Paul, hang on."

Jenkins turned round to see a man jogging towards him. He knew he recognised him but wasn't sure from where. As the man got closer to him, the penny dropped.

"Nick? Is that you?"

"Yeah, how you doing?"

"How am I doing? I'm fucked, Nick. Just come off duty."

"Right. Long one, eh?"

Paul pulled his phone out of his pocket and pretended to check it. He wasn't sure how to act with Nick. It had been a long time since he'd seen him, so long that Paul wasn't even sure on what terms they'd last met.

"It's always a long one, Nick. What is it?"

"What do you mean?"

"Don't fuck about, Nick. Like I said, it's been a fucking long one, I'm frazzled as fuck and I'm not in the mood for this shit right now."

"What shit?"

"Nick, I haven't seen you in fuck knows how long. You haven't turned up here by chance for a quick chat. You're obviously after something, so out with it, then I can get home to bed."

As he said it, Paul knew that this encounter would

ensure he wouldn't be going directly home at its conclusion, but would need a pint first.

"Are you on the murder enquiry?"

"I'm on two murder enquires."

"I mean the kid."

"Which kid?"

"Christian. Christian McGann."

Paul leaned back against his car.

"Why are you asking?"

"It's just... something I'm interested in."

"Interested? In what capacity?"

"A professional one."

Paul took out his cigarettes and lit one up.

"Professional?"

"Yeah."

"Which profession is that, again? Bodyguard or something?"

Nick looked down at the ground.

"Security consultant."

"Right, that's it, yeah. Good money in that, is there?"

"Yeah, it's OK."

"I bet it is. But the question remains: why would a security consultant be interested in the murder of a teenage boy?"

"It's just something I'm... looking into."

"Looking into?"

Nick looked away and nodded his head.

"Again, Nick, the question remains: what the fuck is a private security consultant, Michael Epson's right-hand man, or lapdog, or whatever the fuck it is you are to him, doing 'looking into' the murder of a local teenager?"

"Look, Paul. It's a long story, it's just something I've got a professional interest in. I just wanted to know how the investigation was going, if there's anything you can tell me. That's all."

Paul took a last, long drag on his cigarette and flicked it into the near distance. He took a step closer to Nick and lowered his voice.

"Here's something I can tell you about *my* investigation, Nick. Now, I've got no idea what the fuck you're up to, but if you know even the slightest thing, or have even the smallest bit of info about it, then you'd better fucking tell me. And if I found out you've in any way interfered with, disrupted or withheld information from *my* investigation, then I promise you I'll do everything I can to ruin you, and I don't give a fuck who you're friends with. Do you understand me?"

"I understand."

"Christian McGann was seen on CCTV with a large, muscular man with very short hair in the city centre about three hours before his estimated time of death."

Paul turned away towards his car.

"Is that it?"

Paul took a step back towards Nick.

"Listen, you're lucky I'm sharing that much with you. Exactly what the fuck did you think you were gonna get from me? Are you under the impression there's some sort of professional courtesy between us? Because there isn't, mate. You haven't been a cop for years. And even when you were, you weren't much of one. In fact, you were a fucking disgrace of a police officer, from what I remember of you. Which isn't much. Now, judging by your fancy suit and flash car, it looks like you've done very well for yourself doing whatever the fuck it is you do, so why don't you just stick to that and leave the police work for the rest of us? Now, if you don't mind, I'm going home."

Before Nick could reply, he was walking back to his car. Nick walked back into his own car and shut the door. Fuck Paul Jenkins. Fuck him. Arrogant fucking cunt. Nick knew more than he did already. Paul made no mention of Christian being gay. When he mentioned Epson he clearly had no idea about Epson and Christian knowing each other. So Nick was already ahead of them. He didn't need their fucking help. He'd find the killer himself, before the police did.

Jenkins angled his rear-view mirror so he could watch Hanman walking back to his car, a white Range Rover. Hanman sat inside for a minute, and seemed to be talking to himself. Not talking to himself, no. Arguing with himself. Paul took out his phone and dialled.

"Yes, sir?"

"Johnson, that Berry death."

"The what, sir?"

"Francis Berry. Gambia Terrace. You know, the queer sex game gone wrong?"

"Oh yeah. What about it, sir?"

"On the door-to-door, there was mention of a car seen hanging around about the time of death. What kind of car was it?"

A pause, followed by the sound of Johnson flicking through his notepad.

"A large Range Rover type. White or light in colour."

Jenkins looked back in his rear-view as Hanman pulled away.

"That's what I thought."

"Erm, is everything alright, sir?"

"I dunno, Johnson." Jenkins let the line go silent for a moment. "Forget it, it's nothing. See you tomorrow."

"Yes, sir."

Jenkins was about to end the call, but put the phone back to his ear.

"Johnson? You still there?"

"Sir."

"Look, this may be nothing, but find out everything you can about a fella called Nick Hanman for me, will you? Ex-copper, runs a security firm in town now. Email it over to me when you're done."

Jenkins ended the call and weighed up his options once more. He started the engine, and headed for home.

*

Nick sat in his car, parked about five doors down from the house where Christian McGann had lived with his parents until a few days ago. The house where Nick himself had picked Christian up, and driven him to the hotel, just a couple of weeks ago. He leaned back in his seat and pulled a box of diazepam from his pocket, popped a couple of tablets from their blister packet and threw them into his mouth. He turned to his left, and Francis was staring at him.

"What the fuck do you want, Francis?"

Francis said nothing, just stared back at Nick.

"What? Is you turning up like this from time to time supposed to make me feel bad or something? You've got the wrong guy, if that's the case."

Still he said nothing.

"Look, you made your choices, Francis. If you hadn't have made those choices, then things might have turned out very differently for you. But you did, so here you are, sitting in my fucking car, trying to make me feel sorry for you. Well, you're wasting your time, mate. Now, fuck off, will you? I'm busy."

Nick turned back to watch the front door of Christian's house. When he turned back, Francis was still there, but he wasn't looking at Nick this time. He was staring at the front door of the house.

"Oi!" Nick said. "Oi, what the fuck are you looking at? What the fuck are you trying to achieve?"

Francis ignored him and arched his neck to get a better view.

"Stop that. Stop looking at his house. This is none of your business. Just... just fucking get lost, will you? Oi!"

Still Francis ignored him, stretching himself up further in his seat, arching his neck like a curious meerkat.

"I said stop looking at his house."

Nick scrunched his eyes together tightly and rubbed them with his palms. When he opened them, Francis was finally gone.

"Fucking annoying cunt," he muttered to himself.

He reached into his pocket and took out his cigarettes. As he put one in his mouth someone passed by the passenger-side window, heading towards the house. The man approached the gate and turned up the path. Nick put the ciggie away and got out of the car, reaching the path just as the man was about to turn the key in the door.

"Mr McGann?"

He stopped and turned towards Nick. His eyes were red, his skin pale. He looked like he hadn't slept in days.

"Yeah?"

"I wondered if I could have a word with you, please. About Chris."

*

Billy McGann hung his coat in the hallway and motioned for Nick to pass into the living room. As Nick passed by him he caught the familiar whiff of booze on his skin. Not fresh booze – Nick surmised he probably hadn't come straight from the pub; this was days-old booze smell. The kind that slowly sweated itself out of your pores when you'd been going at it for a while without any real let-up. Nick knew this was probably the soberest Billy McGann had been for a while, and was likely to be for a while longer yet.

"Have a seat," he said, gesturing towards the couch. Nick sat down and Billy took a seat in the corner opposite him.

"Is Mrs McGann home?"

"No, she's round at her sister's place. She's been... it's all been... it's best for her to be there at the minute, I think."

Nick followed Billy's eyes to the mantelpiece. One framed picture of the three of them, Chris aged about seven or eight. A quick scan of the room revealed a few more pictures of him, school portraits, mostly, a couple more family snaps, but nothing recent.

"I understand."

Billy blinked away a few tears.

"So, what was it you wanted to ask me, then?"

"Just a few basic questions about Chris's movements in the days before... the days before. His habits, routines, et cetera."

Billy rolled himself a cigarette and lit it up.

"Basic questions? We've been over all the basic questions a dozen times already. And the complicated ones. Why are you coming back asking the same shit we've answered already?"

"It's just to make sure nothing's been overlooked. I'm

just being thorough."

Billy shook his head and took a drag of his rollie.

"I'll tell you exactly what I told the others. His habits hadn't changed. His behaviour hadn't changed. He went to college. He went out with his mates. When he was at home, he was usually in his room, blasting out that awful fucking music he listens to. Listened to. We saw him mostly at meal times. He didn't say or do anything he didn't normally say or do."

"What about his friends?"

"What about them? He had a bunch that would knock round for him sometimes. Few lads, few girls. I didn't even know their names, most of them. Sour-faced bunch, really. They'd be up in his room with him, but mostly he met them out in town."

"Did he have a girlfriend?"

"Not that I know of."

Nick hesitated before asking his next question, and readied himself for the reaction.

"Boyfriend?"

Billy stubbed his rollie out and instantly made another one. He took a deep drag of it and settled back into his chair.

"You're the first one to have picked up on that," he said quietly.

"So Chris did have a boyfriend?"

"I don't fucking know. I never saw anything to make me think any of the lads he had coming round were more than friends."

"So, how did you..."

"How did I know?" He looked up at the photo on the mantelpiece. "I don't know. A dad just knows things, I suppose. There doesn't have to be any signs or whatever. You just pick up on certain things. Mums too, most likely, but I never spoke to his mum about it. A dad just knows, I reckon, if his son's a, you know..."

Nancy boy. Shirt-lifter. Poof. Faggot. Queer.

Billy reached down the side of his chair and produced a half-empty bottle of whiskey and a glass. Nick got a quick flash of his own father, sitting in his chair, in his corner, a bottle of whiskey permanently at the side of the chair. Billy poured himself a dram and took a swig. He lifted the bottle towards Nick. Nick paused but held up his hand.

"No, not while you're on duty and all that." He knocked his own measure back and poured himself another.

"Erm... I'm not actually on duty."

"How do you mean?"

"Mr McGann, I'm not exactly with the police."

Billy's face darkened in an instant, and he leaned forward in his chair.

"You what? Who the fuck are you with, then?"

Nick didn't know quite what to say. He hadn't even expected to get in the front door, and hadn't really thought how to explain himself. Billy stood up and grabbed Nick by the collar, slamming him against the wall.

"You fucking bastard, you're a fucking reporter, aren't you?"

"No, I'm not," Nick said, lifting his hands up, "I'm honestly not a reporter."

"THEN WHAT THE FUCK ARE YOU? WHAT ARE YOU DOING IN MY FUCKING HOUSE? WHO ARE YOU?"

Nick reached into his pocket and pulled out a business card and handed it to Billy. Billy took it in one hand and softened his grip on Nick with the other.

"'Nick Hanman. Hanman Total Security Solutions'. What the fuck does that mean? *Who are you?*"

Billy's red eyes were filled with anger and confusion.

"I'm a private security consultant. I used to be in the police but I do security, consultancy, investigation..."

"What, like a private detective?"

"Sort of, yeah."

"So, you're what? Looking for fucking business? What the fuck is wrong with you?" His grip on Nick tightened again. "Do I look like I can afford a private detective? And is this how you get your fucking business? Turning up at people's homes when their kids have been... have been fucking murdered?"

"No, Mr McGann, it's not like that. I'm not after your

money. I'm just... I'm looking into Chris's murder."

"*WHY? WHAT THE FUCK DO YOU CARE?*"

"It's complicated."

"*WERE YOU FUCKING HIM? IS THAT IT?*"

"No, I promise you, it's nothing like that. I just... we met, that's all. I met him and... then I saw what had happened to him, and I wanted to help. I don't think the police are taking it seriously enough, and I wanna help. I wanna catch the bastard that did this, that's all."

Billy let go of him and turned away.

"And can you?"

"I don't know. But I'm gonna try. I'm gonna give it everything I've got."

"Why is it so important to you? You barely knew him."

"I've got fuck all else."

Billy turned to face him, and looked him up and down.

"No. I can see that."

He walked back to his chair and sat down, downing the whiskey.

"So what the fuck are you still doing here? You wanna find him, go and fucking find him."

Nick didn't say anything. He straightened himself up and left the living room, closing the door behind him.

As he reached the front door, he heard Billy McGann crying.

*

Nick opened the door to his office suite slowly. He half expected Epson to have had it emptied and the locks changed. The guy on the front desk had greeted him as usual, which was surprising enough in itself; Nick had pretty much assumed security would have been told not to let him in the building. He flicked the light on to see that nothing had actually changed. Kathleen's desk was empty, but there were a couple of pens on the desk and the calendar showed today's date. He walked over to the door behind her desk, leading into his private office area. It was open, as he'd left it. The motion-detector lights flickered on as he entered. Kathleen had had a tidy around; otherwise, things were as he'd left them. He sat down on the couch and picked up the remote control to flick on the Bose with the iPod docked on it. Springsteen's "The River" blasted out from it. He turned the sound down, closed his eyes, leaned back on the couch and tried to think. He tried to piece together what he knew, but it was so long since he'd had to think like this. It was over a decade since he left the force, and even when he was still on it he'd never investigated anything like this. He rubbed his temples and tried to *focus*, but there was too much chatter in his head. All he could see was Chris's face, battered beyond recognition, interspersed with Monica's face, looking at him imploringly, all of it mixed up with The Boss's harmonica. *"They bring you up to do like your daddy done"*. He switched the music off and stood up. He took a thick marker pen from his desk. He pulled the drawers out looking for a large sheet of paper but, finding nothing bigger than A4 size, he walked to the largest wall in the office. It was covered with framed photographs of Nick with all kinds of celebrities; footballers, musicians, politicians, actors. He knocked every one of them to the floor, until the wall was a blank canvass. He crunched them all underfoot as he wrote *CHRISTIAN MCGANN* in six-inch-high letters right in the centre. From his name he drew a line, then another, and another. At the end of each line he wrote what he knew, thought he knew, or needed to know about him: *GAY. LARGE MUSCULAR MAN — SHORT HAIR. RENT BOY?* He wanted to put a line through "rent boy". He didn't like to think of Christian in those terms. But he didn't have much information to go on, and what he'd witnessed when he picked him up for Epson spoke for itself. Christian fucked for money. He'd done it once that Nick knew of, so he may well have done it other times too. What else? Nick opened the bottom drawer and took out the bottle in there. He took a single, big gulp of it. What else?

"What fucking else?" he yelled.

He remembered the night he'd driven him to the hotel. He offered to drive him home but Christian insisted on being dropped off in town. Said he was meeting mates. So he was socially active late at night. *NIGHTCLUBS.* He remembered Epson had found him online. An app called Grindr, he remembered. *GRINDR.*

He swigged some more of the whiskey, grabbed his phone and downloaded the Grindr app. He set up a profile so he could search for men active on the site in the last week in Liverpool and nearby. He scrolled through the search results. Most of them were fit, young guys, late teens, early twenties. A few camp, old queens, all looking out of place and like they were struggling to get to grips with the new technology, Nick seeing in their eyes a hint of bitterness that this kind of social-networking app wasn't around when they were young. Even their poses and pouts looked desperate. Nick saw the appeal of that facet of the gay lifestyle. He admired it a little. They knew what they wanted and sought out similarly inclined individuals. Everyone in it for exactly the same thing. No exploitation, everyone knows where they stand, everyone just getting exactly what they need. And now, with apps like this, they could even negate the need to go to some dingy club. They could obtain everything they needed without ever leaving their homes. A brave new world of no-strings-attached fucking. But none of these faces fitted what he was looking for. He was about to delete the app when one username caught his eye: "Beast". Nick clicked on his profile and his profile pictures. He was muscular, almost body-builder proportions. Each picture was a mirror "selfie" showing his body from different angles. He didn't show his face clearly, only a partial side profile, but Nick could see he was shaven-headed. Nick checked his profile details. It said he was looking for "teen sluts" and his preferences were "dominance" and "rough play". Bald, muscular. An undercurrent of violence. And the name. It fit, but Nick knew the odds must be tiny. But there was a feeling he had, it just *fit.* The locator on the app told Nick where Beast was. Stanley Street. Nick did a quick search of the gay bars there. Only one was open now. Superstar Boudoir. Nick grabbed his coat.

THIRTY-TWO

Scott parked up in the NCP multi-storey car park a few hundred yards away from the club. There were some parking spaces round the back of the club but he didn't want to run the risk of being seen there. He snorted a quick line off the dashboard of his car and got out. He pulled his hat on and zipped his jacket up as far over his face as he could before walking round the block to the club.

"You know what kind of club this is, don't you?" the bouncer asked him as he got to the door. Scott vaguely recognised his face but he wasn't someone he knew, and the hat and jacket were probably enough to put the bouncer off even if he would have recognised Scott. Likewise the other two guys on the door.

"Yeah, I know," he muttered without making full eye contact or looking up, and stepped through the door. As soon as it closed behind him he took the hat and jacket off. Now he was inside, he was free to be what he wanted, free to be The Beast. He put his coat in the cloakroom and headed to the bar and ordered a double vodka and Red Bull. He leaned against the bar and sipped it slowly. He surveyed the other men there. Plenty of them passing by eyed him up, not being subtle about it. He'd observed this behaviour in these people before. The brazen way in which they stared at each other like pieces of meat. It had always sickened him, and it still did even now. Now though, now it pleased him too. But none of the ones looking at him were what he was looking for. They were too much like him, too big, too muscular. He didn't want to fuck a clone of himself. It wasn't what turned him on, plus, for what he wanted to do, he needed to be able to physically dominate his prey. He needed a clear size and strength advantage over whoever he was to take with him, and he was willing to wait it out and leave unaccompanied tonight if the right person didn't come along.

*

Nick instantly felt out of place in the club. Him wearing his suit and tie, smart as they were, everyone else in here dressed to impress, tight trousers and sleeveless tops being the dominant outfit of choice. He felt self-conscious as he approached the bar, feeling the disapproving looks coming his way. The young barman pointedly ignored him for ten minutes before eventually, reluctantly serving him. Nick ordered two double bourbons, to save him having to go through the same thing again anytime soon. He knocked one back and slowly sipped at the other as he slowly walked around the club, looking for someone who fit the image of "Beast". There was more than one. Big, bald, muscular guys – but without having got a clear look at the face on the Grindr profile, he had no way of knowing. Not for sure. He was able to quickly rule most of them out as they seemed to already be with a partner. Beast was clearly single; the guys here were all with guys their own sort of age, whereas it was quite clear Beast was looking for younger. Much younger.

Nick finished his drink and decided to endure the ignorance of the bar staff to get another one. He made it a triple this time, and leant back on the bar and scanned the club again. Immediately, his eyes were drawn to a figure in the corner. Like the other guys, he fit the profile; the size, the bald head. Nick could only see the back of him, but he was talking to someone else, who was obscured by his bulk. Nick moved round to get a better look, without getting too close. The dance floor was between them, but Nick stepped up onto the edge of the stage to give himself an elevated view. His heart nearly stopped as he got a clearer view of who the guy was talking to; a young man, not even a man really, a lad, a boy. Eighteen, maybe nineteen, tops. Blond hair, a good-looking boy. The man had him almost pinned into the corner of the club, one arm above him, leaning against the wall, standing right in his personal space. The lad wasn't enjoying the attention, though. He was clearly uncomfortable and a couple of times tried to move away. First, the man gently put his other arm across him, blocking his way. The second time, he grabbed him by the arm and physically pushed him back to where he wanted him. Now the boy looked genuinely scared, and his eyes were darting around the club, looking for someone to get him out of this situation. Nick gripped his glass tight. He didn't know what to do. If he intervened in any way, it might blow any chance he had of catching this guy, if it turned out it was who he was looking for, but he knew this kid needed his help. He was rooted to the spot as this boy looked around for help. He took any decision-making out of Nick's hands though by somehow wriggling free from his position and getting away from the big guy, who turned towards him and shouted after him. Just one word, Nick couldn't hear it over the music, but he could see clearly enough what the word was. *Faggot.*

The man took a look around then headed for the exit. Nick downed his drink and followed him out, edging out of the door to see him turning the corner. Nick ran to the corner and looked round carefully, just in time to see the man heading into the NCP car park. Nick sprinted full pelt back to his car in the nightclub car park and drove round towards the NCP, parking a hundred yards down the road and hoping he wasn't too late. Within seconds a car pulled out, Nick couldn't see the driver clearly but quickly calculated the chances of anyone else pulling out at this time of night, gave it a few more seconds to see if anyone else was coming out, and followed him. As he reached the out ramp of the NCP he slammed on his brakes and looked up to see if any other cars were coming down. He kept one eye on the ramp and one on the car that had left. With no other cars in view inside the car park and the one car about to turn the corner and out of view, he decided he had to take a chance and hope his instincts were right, otherwise he'd lose him and be back at square one. He took off after the car and followed it at a discreet distance. The guy, if it was the guy he'd seen in the club, was edgy as fuck, clearly high on something, and so could possibly be hyperaware of someone following him. Nick tailed him through Allerton, past the bars and restaurants, before he pulled up outside a mid-sized semi-detached. Nick tucked in halfway down the street and killed his engine and lights. The driver got out. From where he was, Nick couldn't see much detail, but he could see enough – the huge frame, the bald head – to know he had followed the right car. The front door of the house slammed and a light came on inside. After counting to one hundred, Nick started his engine up again and slowly approached the house, leaving his lights off. Idling in the street outside, he assessed the front of the house, getting an overview of the layout, and writing down the make and reg number of the car. As he prepared to pull away, he thought he saw a curtain flutter on the top floor of the house. He looked up at the window, wondering, if he was looking out, how much detail he would be able to see. He let the handbrake off and pulled away as normally as he could.

Inside the house, Scott watched the car pull away. No lights on, it was dark outside and the car wasn't close to the street lights. He could barely make out the shape of the car, never mind what the driver looked like. He watched it pull away, telling himself he was being paranoid, that the car had probably just been a drunk driver or a cabbie who'd forgotten to switch his lights on.

But he knew. Deep down, he knew. The driver had been watching his house. Watching him.

THIRTY-THREE

One last try. He knew he had to give it one last try. Despite everything, he owed it to Monica and to Lisa. Himself, he wasn't so sure about. Still, the locks hadn't been changed. Not yet, at least. He stepped into the house and heard the sound of the television coming from the living room. He turned the corner and saw the two of them huddled up together on the couch. Lisa with her legs up, Monica curled up in front of her like a teddy bear, Lisa's arm draped over her.

"Hi," he said, because he couldn't think of anything else to say.

"Daddy's home," Monica shouted, lifting Lisa's arm up and instantly running round the couch to him. He knelt down and opened his arms for her to run into. "Where've you been, Daddy? We haven't seen you for aaaages."

"I know, Daddy's been very busy. Had to work lots and lots."

"Are you staying with us now?"

Nick saw Lisa rising from the couch now.

"Probably not, baby. I've still got lots of work to do. I might have to go away for a while again."

"Aww, but you've just got back."

"I know, I'm sorry."

"Can I show you the painting I did at school?"

"OK, why don't you go and find it while I talk to Mummy?"

Monica ran off, her little feet thundering up the stairs with the eagerness only a four-year-old on a mission was capable of.

"There's nothing to talk about," Lisa said.

"There is, Lisa. You can't just shut me out of my own family like this."

"Nick, you shut yourself out. I'm not sure how much you were ever really in in the first place. But now, you're just... gone."

"Lisa, please. Try to understand what I'm going through, what's going on."

"I know exactly what's going on, Nick. You're an addict. An alcoholic, a drug addict. And you're an abuse victim. And it breaks my heart what you went through as a child, but I can't help you overcome that, and everything else, until you let me."

"Yes, you're right. I know I'm those things. But that's not what's going on. Not right now. There's something else. Something to do with work. There's a case..."

"A case? Nick, you don't have 'cases'. You're not a cop. You have clients. Clients who you spend more time with than your own family."

"Yes, but this is different. This one, this... matters. It's important. It's... if I can fix this, then –"

"Then what? It'll somehow make things better? Between us?"

"No, it's not that simple, I know that, but I just need to get through this one, then I can make things better. I know it won't be easy, but if you just let me get hold of this – "

"For fuck's sake, Nick! Will you listen to yourself? A few days ago, I kicked you out of here because you've left me no alternative. Because you were always either drunk or high, or focussed on work. And what do you do to try and fix things? You turn up here, drunk, and talking about work. What the hell is the matter with you? When is the penny gonna drop with you, Nick? What will it take to get through to you?"

"Please, Lisa."

"Never mind 'please'. It's no good, Nick. You shouldn't have come here. Just leave."

Nick held up his hands but said nothing. He knew there was nothing more to be said. He turned and headed to the front door. As he got near it, he heard Monica's footsteps coming down the stairs.

"Daddy, I've got my painting."

He kept walking to the front door.

"Wait, Daddy, don't you want to see my picture?"

Nick walked faster, almost running to the door.

"Daddy!"

He opened the door, and without looking back he closed it. Before he slammed it shut, he could hear Monica beginning to cry. He sprinted to his car and sped away.

*

Nick signed into the Cedar visitors' book and headed to his dad's room. The door was open and John was dozing in the big chair in the corner. Nick quietly walked in and sat down opposite him. He watched his father sleeping. He watched the fluttering of the eyelids, the sleepy twitching of his hand, the one weakened by his strokes, the tiny trickle of drool forming at the corner of his mouth. For a full three minutes, Nick sat there and watched his father, seventy-five years old. An old man now. Weakened by age, time and two strokes. And here was Nick; younger, stronger, richer and more powerful. But, even with the old man unconscious, Nick was acutely aware of the huge imbalance of power between the two of them. Physically, there would be nothing to stop Nick taking a pillow from the bed and holding it over John's face. With his left side significantly weakened, even if he woke up and struggled, he would be no match for Nick's superior strength. But, sitting here now, watching his old man sleep, Nick was still as afraid of him as he had been as a weak little boy. Which, in the company of his father, was all he still was.

As though he had sensed himself being watched, maybe even felt the thoughts Nick was having, John suddenly opened his eyes and jumped slightly in his chair. His eyes passed across Nick then, briefly, disorientedly, around the room, before settling back on Nick.

"Oh," he said, rubbing his eyes and reaching for a glass of water, "you're here."

"Yeah."

"Wasn't expecting you."

"No."

"'Yeah'. 'No'. Fucking chatty as always."

Nick said nothing, turning to look out of the window at the grounds.

"So what's happened?"

"What do you mean?"

"Well, you don't show up here unannounced and sit there with a face like a smacked arse unless something has happened. So, come on. Who's died?"

Nick felt like saying "me" but, knowing the derision it'd lead to, stopped himself.

"Nobody."

"So what is it?"

"Lisa. She's kicked me out."

"Again? That's hardly news, is it?"

"For good, this time."

"You've said that before."

"No, it's different this time. It's permanent."

"Well, like I've said before, she always was an uppity cunt, that one."

"Dad!"

"What?"

"Don't... don't say that."

"Don't fucking raise your voice to me, boy."

"I'm not, I just... I wish you wouldn't call her that."

"Right, so she kicks you out and you come here crying to me like a fucking baby. I tell you what she's like and you have a fucking go at me? Tell you what, that bitch really has got her claws properly into you."

Nick jumped up from his chair and leaned into his father's face, a hand on either arm of the chair.

"I said not to talk about her like that."

The slap was so hard it knocked Nick straight to his knees. The left side of his face stung like he'd been hit with a rowing oar. He lifted his hand to it and rubbed it but, aware of how pathetic he must have looked, moved his hand away. His dad was leant forward in his chair, his hand still held up. Whatever strength he now lacked in his left side had, if that slap was anything to go by, been compensated for by the right side.

"You've got some fucking nerve, you have. You come into my flat and dare to fucking talk to me like that. Who the fuck do you think you are?"

Nick fought hard to keep the tears at bay. The last thing he wanted to do after this humiliation was give the bastard the satisfaction of seeing him cry.

"No fucking wonder she kicked you out. Pathetic little weakling. No wonder your mother left you either."

Now there was nothing he could do to stop it, the tears flowed, and the more he tried to stem the flow, the more they came.

"Mum didn't leave – you killed her."

"I killed her? The stupid fucking cow killed herself, you know that."

"Because of what you did to her."

"I did fuck all to her."

"Yes you did. You bullied her, you beat her, you abused her. You wore her down till she felt like she had no choice but to kill herself."

"Bollocks – if anything, she killed herself to get away from you. And who can fucking blame her? Just look at you. With your fancy cars and clothes and house. Trust me, lad, none of it hides what you really are."

"Fuck you!"

John raised his hand as though to slap him again, even though the force of the first slap had knocked Nick well out of his reach. That didn't stop Nick from instinctively flinching. John noticed it and simply shook his head in disgust. He put his hand down.

"Just fucking get out of here," he said. "Get out and don't bother fucking coming back. Keep paying my bills, keep the spending money coming, but stay the fuck away from here."

Nick didn't move for a second.

"Go on," his father said, turning away and switching the television on. "Just fucking get out."

He didn't look back in his son's direction, looking

instead at whichever daytime quiz show was on. Nick picked himself up off the floor, took one last look at his dad, and walked out of Cedar Nursing Home.

*

Michael held the phone receiver in his hand, his finger poised above the call button. He had dialled the number, he just had to connect the call now, but he hesitated. He slammed the phone back into the receiver and walked away from his desk. This was the third time he'd attempted to make the call now, but as yet he'd been unable to do so. Such hesitation was deeply uncharacteristic of him. Usually, if something needed to be done, he did it. If it was necessary, he wasn't afraid of making tough decisions. Never had been. You didn't get to the position he was in without being able to make the kinds of choices lesser men would wrestle with. Michael had always been clinical in thought and action. Brutal, even. But now, he was torn. He walked to the window and looked out over the city. His city. He weighed up his options again. But he knew there were few if any options. Nick had to go. He knew too much, had done too much on his behalf, to have him go off the reservation now. Nick had always been unstable. It was exactly this instability which allowed Michael to manipulate him so easily. He'd had meltdowns before. In fact, Nick's life seemed to be one long meltdown. But this time was different. The fact that Nick had raised his hand to him. Actually hit him. Not that Michael was in any way surprised at Nick's capacity for violence – he also knew that, relatively speaking, what Nick had done was very low on the register. It was a clumsy slap rather than a punch or anything harder. But it had been at *him*. Nick had barely disagreed with Michael before, now he was attacking him. In his own office. When Michael looked into Nick's eyes that day, he knew he was gone. The anger – that was always there, but what he saw when he raised his hand was much worse. It was the look of a man who had nothing left to lose. Michael had seen it coming, with the ignored phone calls, the storming out of his office. He cursed himself now for not acting sooner. Things could have been contained, one way or the other, had he acted sooner; there may have been other avenues to explore. Now he was left with no choice. He knew that. His hand had been forced. The only other option was to use Nick's family as leverage, but Michael was not prepared to do that. That was a line he was not prepared to cross. Which left one course of action alone. So why was he hesitating? His relationship with Nick was complex. Not quite friends, not quite paternal, not quite boss/employee. They'd been through a lot together. Michael had seen Nick go from scared, young copper to what he was now; still scared, still messed up, but able to present something very different to the world. In the eyes of most people, Nick was now a powerful and successful man. And Nick had seen Michael go from bog-standard successful businessman to practically owning this city. And they had helped each other get to their respective summits. They'd shared secrets with each other that nobody else knew. And that was what made Nick so dangerous now. A man with that much knowledge, who thinks he has nothing left to lose? There was no telling the damage he could wreak. Michael took one last, long look at the Liverpool skyline, crossed the floor back to his desk, and made the call.

*

Nick banged on the door. He heard the male voice on the other side of the door, then Sally's as she approached. She opened the door a crack.

"Nick?"

"Hi, Sally. Can I come in?"

"No, not right now. I'm busy, Nick."

"I need to see you. Can't you get rid of him?"

"No, I can't. You'll have to come back later."

Nick pushed the door open, knocking Sally back into the hallway.

"Oi!" Sally shouted as Nick stormed into the house, "what the fuck you doing?"

Nick walked into the ground floor bedroom. Nick knew that Sally had a proper bedroom upstairs, but this was where she saw her clients. A middle-aged man with a gut and hairy, fat legs was sitting on the bed, nude. He didn't make any attempt to cover himself as Nick barged in.

"Who the fuck are you?"

"Fuck off," Nick said, picking his trousers up and throwing them at him.

"Nick!" Sally shouted as she followed him in. "Stop this. I'm sorry, Pete."

"Who the fuck is this prick?" he asked, nodding his head at Nick as he stood up, still making no effort to hide his nakedness.

"I'm the guy who's telling you to fuck off. Now."

"I'm not going anywhere, pal. I've paid for the hour and I'm getting the fucking hour."

"No, you're fucking not. Not today. Now are you gonna fuck off now or shall I give your missus a ring?"

"I'm not married, mate. Unlike you," Pete said, nodding at the ring on Nick's finger.

"Nick," Sally shouted. "This isn't on. If anyone's gonna be leaving now, it's gonna be you."

Nick looked round at her, then back to Pete.

"How much?" Nick asked him.

"Eh?"

"How much?"

"How much what?"

"How much have you paid? For the hour?"

Pete narrowed his eyes at Nick, like he was weighing up the question.

"A tonne-fifty," he replied. "I have to pay a bit extra to use the back door, if you know what I mean."

He gave Nick a wink, and Nick had to work hard not to jam his fingers into his eyes.

"Alright, I'll give you three hundred."

"What for?"

"To fuck off for now. Then you can have two hours, on me. But not now."

"Nick," Sally shouted again, "this isn't on. Now you need—"

"It's alright, Sal," Pete interrupted her. "That's a fair deal."

He held his hand out to Nick.

"I'll take the cash now then, if you don't mind."

"For fuck's sake," Sally muttered to herself, shaking her head.

Nick handed the money over and Pete got dressed and left, telling Sally he'd give her a call. Nick heard Sally close the door then storm back through to the bedroom.

"Who the fucking hell do you think you are?"

"Look, I'm sorry, but I needed to see you."

"Well then you make a fucking appointment, like everybody else. Or you at least wait your fucking turn. What the fuck were you thinking? This is my fucking livelihood, Nick. I'll probably never see Pete again now, and he was a regular. He came here at least once a week."

"He'll be back," Nick said dismissively.

"You don't fucking know that. And anyway, that's beside the point. What gives you the fucking right to barge into my house like that?"

"Look, I'm sorry. I'll make it up to you." He was already counting the notes out from his wallet.

"What are you doing?"

Nick dropped a pile of notes onto the bed.

"Four hundred. There's four hundred quid there. With what Pete had paid you, that's not a bad morning's work."

"That's not the point, Nick."

"I know, it won't happen again."

Sally picked the notes up and counted them.

"Alright, fine. Whatever. Let's go."

Down in the basement, the basement that only they used, Nick on his knees, the rope around his neck. He leaned into the rope.

"Hit me," he said to her. And, without hesitation, she did. And again. And she told him what he wanted to hear.

"You dirty, little bastard. You pathetic, worthless, little piece of shit. You fucking disgusting, filthy, ugly, deformed little fucker."

*

Half an hour later, before he reached the front door, Sally

197

called him back.

"What is it?"

"I don't think you should come here again. Not for a while, at least."

"Why?"

Sally looked at him.

"You really need to ask that question, Nick? I just think it'd be best. At least, until you've sorted out whatever it is you've got going on in your head at the moment."

"You fucking serious?"

"Deadly."

"I didn't realise whores had such scruples."

"Oh, that's original. Never been called that before."

"You've got a pretty fucking smart mouth for someone who fucks fat old men like Pete for money."

"Here we go, showing your true fucking colours now, aren't you? Just last week you were my guardian angel, now I'm just a whore. Tell you what, Nick, don't ever bother coming back. Find someone else to do your fucking weird shit for you. I'm sure you won't have any trouble finding some other old slag. Now fuck off out of my house."

Nick just didn't have the energy to argue anymore. He left the house and headed back to the office.

*

He walked into the building foyer and waved to Clive on the desk. Clive beckoned him over.

"Nick," he whispered, leaning in close, "there's a policeman here to see you."

"What policeman?"

"A Detective Sergeant Jenkins."

Clive nodded as discreetly as he could over Nick's shoulder. Nick turned his head to the side to see Jenkins, sitting at an isolated table in the coffee shop, his back to the desk.

"OK, cheers, Clive. Do me a favour, pass me that notepad."

Clive passed it to him and he took out a pen and began scribbling as he approached the coffee shop table. Nick sat down opposite him. Nick finished his pretend paperwork and put the pen down as Jenkins folded up the newspaper he'd been reading.

"What can I do for you, DS Jenkins?"

"I'm gonna get straight to the point. I wanna know what the fuck you're up to."

"Up to?" Nick gestured towards the pad. "At this present moment, a bit of paperwork."

"Don't play fucking games with me, Hanman," Jenkins shouted, slamming his hand on the table. Nick managed not to let his surprise show.

"I don't know what you're—"

"A couple of days ago you showed up at my station asking questions about a murder investigation, with only the vaguest explanation as to why you were interested."

"Look," Nick said, "I saw it on the news, that's all. It sounded like a really nasty case, and I got a bit upset about it. I'd had a few, and I wondered if I could help somehow. It sounds silly now, I know, but that's all there was to it."

Nick had put on his best performance but could see Jenkins wasn't convinced.

"Are you familiar with Francis Berry?"

"Who?"

"Francis Berry. The reason I ask is that a car similar to yours was seen outside his flat the night he died."

Nick shrugged.

"A car *like* mine? There's a lot of cars *like* mine, detective."

"So you didn't know him?"

Nick shook his head.

"So I don't suppose we'd happen to find any of your DNA in his flat if we were to re-examine it?"

Nick held out his wrists.

"What are you doing?"

"Waiting for you to put the cuffs on."

"What?"

"Well," Nick said, "if you're talking about things like DNA, then presumably I'm under arrest, as that's the only

199

way you're going to be getting any DNA samples off me."

"You're not under arrest," Jenkins said through gritted teeth.

"Well, that's a relief. I have to go and visit a client, you see, so if you'll excuse me, I'm on my way out. I am free to leave, aren't I?"

"You're free to leave. Unless there's anything you'd like to tell me."

Nick said nothing.

Jenkins stood up slowly and reached into his coat pocket. He pulled out a business card and held it out to Nick.

"If you think of anything you'd like to talk to me about, perhaps concerning the murder of a local teen, or the death of a local drug dealer" – Nick ignored the card and Jenkins eventually placed it down on top of the newspaper – "then please do give me a call."

He fastened his jacket and began walking towards the door.

"Be seeing you," he said before he went through it.

*

Nick drove up to the top floor of the NCP multi-storey and parked up in the farthest corner. What now? It was nearly eight o'clock and darkness was beginning to fall over the city. He got out of the car and walked to the edge of the roof. He looked down at the streets, the nightlife crowds beginning to form. He took his phone out and clicked on the Facebook app. He typed in Christian McGann and looked through his pictures again. He read the posts on his wall, the tributes, the eulogies. Everything else was gone now. Family, the work. All that remained was Christian. In the absence of anything better to do, he headed round to the city's gay quarter. He wanted to be somewhere where nobody would know him, and went into the dingiest bar he could find. It was dark inside, and there was already a decent-sized crowd of drinkers. He sat at the bar and ordered a pint of lager and a double whiskey. He knocked them both back and ordered more of the same, and kept doing it for the next hour. Eventually, he stumbled downstairs to the toilet. He leant against the wall as he pissed into the urinal, ignoring the guy next to him, who he knew was trying to see over his shoulder. Nick felt the fella back away as Nick finished off. As he turned round, the guy was stood by the door of the toilet cubicle, white T-shirt, shaven head, leather waistcoat, probably a couple of years older than Nick, watching him. As Nick looked over at him, the guy nodded his head towards the cubicle. Nick let out a little chuckle.

"No thanks, mate," he said. "You've got the wrong end of the stick there."

"I don't think so," the guy replied.

Nick hesitated for a moment.

"Fuck it," he said, and followed the guy into the cubicle, and shut the door behind him.

*

Nick staggered back up the stairs to the bar, ordering another pint as he attempted to sit back on the bar stool he had vacated. He misjudged the height of it, though, and slipped to the floor.

"I think you've probably had enough, mate," the barman said.

"Don't be soft, just give us another pint," Nick said, noticing the slurring of his words.

"I don't think so."

"GIVE ME A FUCKING PINT!"

The barman took a step back.

"Right, I think you'd best be on your way now."

"GIVE ME A PINT OF THAT FUCKING QUEER BEER!"

A few other punters starting booing and heckling him at that, and he turned around to face them.

"GET FUCKED! FUCKING COCKSUCKERS!"

By now the two bouncers on the door had come in and grabbed an arm each, and dragged him towards the door, throwing him out into the alley, slamming the doors of the club shut.

"FUCKING BASTARDS!"

He picked up a nearby wheelie bin and threw it against the door before heading out of the alleyway and back to the car park. He slammed his fist against the steering wheel. The horn blared out but he didn't care, he was the only person parked on the roof. He switched on the car stereo as he leant back in his seat, the Hold Steady's "Stay Positive" blasting instantly out. He closed his eyes as he fought back the tears, and tried to focus. What now?

"Woah-oh-oh, woah-oh-oh. We gotta stay positive," sang Craig Finn. Nick ran his fingers through his hair before it hit him. He knew where he should be. It was so obvious; he slapped himself for wasting his time here. He had a suspect – a strong one. So what the fuck was he doing in town getting thrown out of gay bars? He started his engine, but then killed it instantly. He was too drunk, too sloppy, for what he was planning. He flipped open the glove box and took out the little plastic bag at the back of it. He took out three of the little, pink, amphetamine tablets in there and swallowed them, washing them down with the flat remains of a bottle of Coke he picked up from the floor. He decided the drive would be time enough for them to kick in, so turned the engine back on and flew down the ramps of the car park and out of town.

*

By the time he pulled up down the street from the house, he felt like he didn't have a drop of alcohol in his system. He switched off his engine and opened the Grindr app, checking the "Beast" profile. He hadn't logged in for two days. Nick was feeling bold so he leaned across and opened the passenger door, sliding across and out, pushing the door gently shut. Using the other parked cars as cover, he crouched down and walked along the road until he was almost opposite the house. He could see a light on upstairs. While he considered the possibility that the light could have been left on as a deterrent, he saw movement behind the curtain. He quickly made his way back to the car, climbing back in through the passenger door. He dropped back into the driver's seat and leaned back across to close the door, leaning across Francis, who was now sat there.

"Fuck off, Francis," he said as he pulled the door shut. "It's not a good time." By the time he turned back, Francis had already gone.

Nick sat there for another forty minutes. The speed had made him antsy and restless. He wanted to go somewhere and do something else, but if his instincts were right, then this fella was not someone likely to stay in much. Not in a city like this. It seemed worth the wait.

Less than twenty minutes later, he heard a door slam. He lowered himself down in his car seat and watched, and saw him coming out of the front door. He got into his car and drove off. Nick had two options: follow him or break in. He decided he knew where he was likely to be going, and that this might be a one-off opportunity. He waited until he had turned the corner and got out. He looked at the front door; it looked like a pretty simple job, but he decided the back was more sensible – the back yard would give him more cover, unless there was a security light. He walked down the alleyway and round the back. Unsurprisingly, the back gate was locked, so he pulled up a bin and climbed up onto it. He dropped quietly down into the back yard. No security lights went off but he kept low anyway, moving towards the back door. The back door was a single mortis lock. Nick took out his Southord lock-picking set, and it took a full five minutes of fiddling around with his toolkit but, eventually, just as he was about to give up, he managed to unlock it. It led straight into a small kitchen. He closed the door behind him and went inside. Not risking turning the lights on, he turned on the torch on his iPhone, keeping the beam low. On the work surface was a small pile of mail. Nick lifted the top letter up and read the name on it: Scott Collins. Knowing he could be short on time, Nick headed straight upstairs. He wasn't even sure what he was looking for, but he thought it unlikely he'd find much of interest in the living room. He opened the first door upstairs to what looked like a spare room; weights bench, boxes and a single bed covered in clothes. He shut the door and moved on to the next room. This was obviously the main bedroom. He opened the clothes drawers. In the sock drawer, there was a pile of tablet boxes to one side. Nick picked them up and read them, recognising them as steroids. On the other side of the drawer was a plastic bag full of tablets and another one full of white powder. In the wardrobe was nothing but clothes. Under the bed there was nothing except a gym bag. He lifted the pillow and saw nothing. As he was about to put the pillow down something caught his eye. Sticking out of the pillow case was a piece of paper. Nick pulled it out to see it was a page of a newspaper, folded. Folded inside that were three more pages. Nick opened the first one to find a page of the *Liverpool Echo* from a few weeks ago; a report into the discovery of the body of a young man. The next one he picked up was from a few days later, a more detailed report, naming the victim. Christian McGann. The other pages were more of the same, all local press, with one report from a national paper. Nick felt his stomach tighten. It was him. On some level he'd known it all along, as soon as he set eyes on the fucker. Regardless of how remote the chances were, instinct told him he was on the right track. What he'd seen on the Grindr app had all but confirmed it. Now he knew. But he knew there was no way this would hold up in court. He wasn't police, and he'd broken in here illegally. And having a few newspaper reports on something was no proof you'd done it. It was barely evidence, and the way he'd come across it made it meaningless. He put the pages back into the pillow, taking care to get it as close to how he'd found it as possible. That's when he heard the key in the front door.

The door slammed. Nick froze on the spot as he heard movement downstairs, and the footsteps moving towards the stairs. They moved quickly to the top floor of the house. Still, Nick stood, paralysed on the spot. He was caught, and there was nothing he could do. But instead of the bedroom door opening, he heard the bathroom door opening and the light going on, followed by the sound of a stream of piss flowing into the toilet. Finally he was able to move, but where to? He couldn't get out without being seen now, that was out of the question. He couldn't take the guy on, he was too big. So he had to hide. Looking quickly around, there were only two options. He remembered how full the wardrobe was, leaving no room for him, so he dropped and rolled under the bed. A

204

second later the door opened, and he watched as Collins's feet walked across the room towards the drawers. As he fiddled in them, Nick watched his feet and could hear Collins muttering to himself, unintelligible apart from the odd "fuck", but constant. Nick held his breath, then realised he could be stuck here, in a room with a psychopath, indefinitely, so he slowly and silently let the breath out, instead taking slow, quiet breaths and keeping perfectly still. He could feel and hear his heart pounding, so loud he thought it must be filling the room. He began to plan how to escape if and when he was discovered, wondering if he was fast enough to get past him, using the element of surprise to his advantage, but then he was relying on the front door being open to be able to get away quickly enough. What if Collins was now in for the night? Would he fall asleep with Nick under his bed, and could Nick sneak out if that happened? Nick tried to remember if the floorboards were squeaky, but couldn't. But then, just as suddenly as he had entered, Collins left the room, switching the light off as he went. He went back down the stairs and out of the front door, locking it behind him. Nick waited a full five minutes before he even moved out from under the bed. He stayed low and went over to the bedroom window. On the street below, there was a gap in front of the house, the car he had followed home the other night nowhere to be seen. He made his way back downstairs to the back door. He pulled it shut and took out his tools to relock it, then paused. He went back into the house and strode up the stairs back to the bedroom. He took the newspaper cuttings out of the pillow case and laid them out across the bed. He went back downstairs and out of the back door, leaving it wide open.

*

Scott Collins. Scott Collins. Scott Collins.

Nick said the name to himself over and over as he drove back into town. He parked up in the underground car park at work, surprised to find that his pass hadn't been disabled yet. He took his phone and Googled "Scott Collins Liverpool". Thousands of results, but not this guy. Same with Facebook and Instagram. The guy seemed to have no online existence other than the Grindr profile. But it didn't matter. Nick knew by now where he was likely to be.

Nick paid the entry fee at Superstar Boudoir and went in. Straight away, he spotted Collins talking to a younger guy near the bar. Nick felt his heart go again, and went to move round the opposite side of the club, out of sight, but then remembered that Collins hadn't actually seen him. Although barely half an hour ago Nick had been just feet away from Collins, in his own bedroom, Collins didn't even know Nick existed. Secure in the knowledge, Nick bought a drink and stood almost next to him and the guy he was chatting to. It was too loud to hear what he was saying, but Nick stood and watched him, watching the back of him. He noticed the detail and definition of his back muscles, the breadth of his shoulders, the thickness of his upper arms. He had already figured this out, but looking at him now, he realised with greater certainty that he was going to have to think of something, a way to deal with him, because, although Nick could fight, he wouldn't stand a chance against this beast.

Suddenly Collins and the other guy moved and left the club. Nick again gave it a few seconds before following them. He couldn't see them when he exited the club but when he looked around the corner he saw them turning into the car park round the back. Nick gave them a couple of minutes to get to Collins's car and either leave, in which case Nick knew where they were likely to be going, or to get up to whatever they were going to be doing. After two minutes it was clear they weren't going anywhere. Nick edged round the corner and saw Collins's car parked in the corner. Keeping close to the wall, he moved towards it, close enough to be able to see the silhouettes of the two men inside, on the back seat. The car rocked slightly as Nick could make out the hulking figure, the much smaller guy pinned under him. He moved closer, close enough to hear what he was saying.

"Fucking queer. Fucking dirty faggot. Fucking cunt," followed by the unmistakable sound of a few slaps. Again he found himself frozen to the spot. He knew that if he acted now, he was unprepared. He hadn't thought it through, and intervening now would probably blow any chance of taking Collins down. But he knew this man had to be stopped, and he was going to do it. He just had to figure out how.

Nick backed away and out of the car park. He headed back to the underground car park of his office building. As he was about to put the key in his car door, he heard a voice.

"Don't move."

Nick stopped and turned slowly around. Six feet away, there was a man, black leather jacket and gloves on, aiming a gun at him.

"Move away from vehicle."

Nick clocked the accent; Ukrainian? Chechen maybe. Not that it mattered, the fucker was pointing a gun at him, it mattered fuck all whether he was from Bulgaria or Basingstoke.

"Who are you?" Nick asked.

"Does it matter?"

"It matters to me."

"If I tell you my name, it makes no difference. You don't know me, I don't know you."

"Presumably we have a mutual acquaintance though?"

The man shrugged his shoulders.

"Who is it?"

The man said nothing.

"Michael Epson," Nick said.

Again the guy kept silent, but Nick spotted a flicker in his eyes, enough to confirm his suspicions.

"I take it you haven't been sent here as a warning?"

"No."

"So just fucking shoot me then."

"Not here. Come, move away from car."

"Come and get me, you fucking goulash-eating cunt."

"Goulash? Wrong country my friend."

"Fucking cabbage, then. And I'm not your friend, you fucking KGB reject."

The man almost smiled.

"If you think you can provoke me into making some sort of mistake, you—"

"CATCH!" Nick yelled, throwing his keys towards the man's face. Instinctively, he moved his hands up to catch them, still holding the gun. Nick was instantly on top of him, rugby-tackling him to the ground. Nick grabbed his head and slammed it into the concrete three times. He saw his grip loosen slightly on the gun and sank his teeth into the hand that held it. The man cried out and Nick felt a punch to the side of his head, though it was more like a blow from a mallet. He had never felt a punch quite like it, and thought he would pass out. He managed to swing his right elbow into the side of his foe's head twice, then repositioned himself on his side, his body weight almost entirely on the arm that still just held the gun at the end of it. A hand gripped Nick's throat and began to tighten. He felt himself beginning to pass out, and threw his head back as hard as he could, feeling the back of it connect with something; nose or cheekbone, he wasn't sure which, but it was enough to loosen the grip on his throat. He grabbed the index and ring fingers of the gun hand and pushed them back, snapping them. Finally the gun came loose and clattered against the floor, and Nick threw his head back a few more times and kicked his legs back against whatever was there. Finally the guy went limp enough for Nick to roll away, grabbing the gun as he went, making sure he rolled far enough to be out of reach, and able to turn and aim the gun. The guy was already holding his hand up, two fingers on his left hand pointing out at an obscene angle. Nick stood up.

"How much?" Nick asked.

"What?"

"How much was he paying you?"

"Why?"

"I wanna know how much my life's worth."

"Probably less than you'd think."

"I fucking doubt that."

The man looked confused.

"I'm guessing English humour doesn't translate too well to Russia, then?"

"Georgia."

"Whatever." Nick took a few more steps back. "Go."

He nodded, and slowly lifted himself off the ground. He began walking towards the entry ramp, but stopped and turned back.

"Nothing personal, OK? Just business."

"You came to fucking kill me. It doesn't get much more personal than that, you cunt. Now piss off, before I change my mind and put a fucking bullet through your face."

THIRTY-FOUR

The first thing Scott noticed as he closed the front door was the cold. Then he heard the sound coming from the kitchen, a tapping noise. Then again, a few seconds later. He gripped his keys tightly in his fist, the house key and car key sticking out from between his fingers as an improvised knuckle-duster. He walked to the kitchen and switched on the light, ready to act. There was nobody there. He was about to switch the light off when he heard the noise again, coming from the back of the kitchen. He moved towards it and saw it was the back door, blowing in the breeze. Panic hit him. Had he left it open? Could he have been that stupid? No. No chance. He had shut it. But wait – he had put the bin out earlier, not long before going out. It's possible he could have forgotten to close it. No, no, he hadn't. No fucking way. Since he'd seen that car outside the house, the driver watching him, he'd been taking extra care. He looked at the sideboard. There was a jar full of pound coins and fivers. His petty cash jar. It was untouched. Over on the kitchen table was his iPad. No burglar would have missed those. His expensive leather jacket was hanging by the front door, he had seen it when he came in. He went through to the living room and switched the light on. The TV was still there, the DVD player beneath it. On the coffee table was the laptop. The relief washed over him and he exhaled deeply. But this was unacceptable. Leaving the back door open like that, that was unacceptable. He hadn't spent all this time training his body, turning himself into The Beast, to go and fuck up like that. If he could make mistakes here, he could make them elsewhere too. Was it the drugs? Maybe he was doing too much coke. No, that wasn't it. The opposite in fact. The drugs were keeping his mind sharp. The little edge of paranoia it brought, he was channelling that to keep himself limber.

Whatever, it couldn't happen again.

After making doubly sure everywhere was secure, he went upstairs. He went into his bedroom and put the bag of pills back in the drawer and was about to go to the spare room to do some weights when he saw something that made the world stop. On the bed. His collection of newspaper cuttings, the ones he kept in his pillow case, were all laid out on top of the duvet. He stood and stared at them as though he was waiting for them to speak to him, to offer some sort of explanation. For a full minute he stared, as he felt his blood bubbling inside him, his heart thumping like he'd just done an intense session at the gym. Every muscle tightened. He left the room and went into the spare room, grabbing a barbell from the floor.

"WHERE ARE YA?" he yelled, marching back into his room. "WHERE THE FUCK ARE YA, YA CUNT? FUCKING COME ON, THEN, LET'S FUCKING HAVE YA!"

He opened the wardrobe, pulling the clothes out, he flipped the mattress from the bed onto the floor.

"FUCKING SHOW YOURSELF, THEN!"

Into the bathroom, he ripped the shower curtain off.

"WHERE THE FUCK ARE YA?"

Down into the living room again, he looked behind the couch, in the tiny cupboard under the stairs. Nothing. No one. Into the kitchen, he flipped the table over.

"FUCKING BASTARDS! FUCKING CUNTS!"

Back into the living room again.

"COME ON, THEN! I'M FUCKING HERE, WHERE ARE YOU?"

He threw the barbell, sending it crashing into the TV, shattering it. He dropped to his knees, tried to get control of his breathing.

"Fuck. Fuck. Fuck."

He told himself to get a grip. Told himself he was The Beast. That nobody fucked with The Beast. He stood up and paced the room. Then he paced the ground floor. Then he paced the whole house. He didn't know what else to do, so he grabbed his keys and left the house. He was about to open the car door when he heard the engine. He looked up to see the car, lights off, coming towards him. Before he had time to react he was airborne. He hardly even felt the impact as he flew up the bonnet and over the roof. The thing that really hurt was when he hit the road. As he did, he heard the car screech to a halt, then reverse back towards him. He lifted his arms up instinctively to protect himself but the car stopped just short of hitting him. Through his blurred vision, he saw feet walking towards him. He looked up to see who it was but all he saw was the foot coming towards his face, then blackness.

*

The nightshift at Cedar Nursing home was unpredictable. Anna had worked here for over seven years and she still didn't know what to expect from one night to the next. Some nights, they'd all be asleep by nine and you wouldn't hear a thing from any of the residents until early the next morning. Some nights, you wouldn't be able to sit down for more than five minutes without an alarm going, someone shouting or screaming. Tonight was one of the quiet ones. Other than the hourly checks, there had been nothing to do all night. Now she was doing the midnight check, nothing more than a rudimentary glance round the corner to make sure everything was as it should be in most cases, a bit more in-depth in others. As she quickly poked her head round John Hanman's door, she hardly even looked at the room. John was pretty much entirely self-sufficient and, what little help he did need, he usually asked for. So Anna only just noticed the empty bed, the cover hanging half on the bed, half onto the floor. Assuming he'd gone to the loo, she opened the bathroom door, but the light was off. Switching it on confirmed her worst fears – John wasn't there. She looked up and noticed the open patio doors and nearly lost control of her bowels.

*

John couldn't move his arms or his legs. His eyes opened slowly, straining against the harsh light. He looked down and saw that he was tied to a chair, his legs tied to the front legs of it, his arms tied to his side by rope that wrapped round his torso and round the back of the chair. He looked around the room. It looked like a garage. No, not a garage, more like one of those storage facilities. He'd seen the kind of place on the TV show where they bid on things that people have left in them. What the fuck was going on? All he remembered was going to sleep, then being woken by a noise in his room. In the dark, he felt something going over his mouth, a chemical smell, then, the next thing he knew, he was waking up here. He heard a sound behind him, a groan of some sort. He turned his head as much as he could to the right. Behind him, to the right, there was another man. He was on a metal chair which looked like it had been screwed or bolted into the floor. He was tied in the same way as John, but with layers of gaffer tape also covering his limbs and torso, as well as the rope. The man was big, really big, but he didn't look like he was going anywhere anytime soon. He was covered in blood, his bald head and face scuffed, and some blood dripping slowly onto the floor from under the restraints. A strip of tape covered his mouth, muffling the sounds he was making, but he was clearly in pain. He eventually opened his own eyes, looking around the room. John saw the same confusion that he himself had felt registering in this man's eyes. His eyes passed around the room till he saw John.

"Who the fuck are you?" John asked.

"Mmmfm hmm mmm rrr uummm."

"Well that didn't fucking tell me much. Don't suppose there's any point asking you where the fuck we are, is there?"

The man stared blankly at John before continuing to look around the room. He began struggling against his restraints, trying to move his chair.

"No good doing that, mate," John said, turning his head away. "I don't think either of us is going anywhere."

Still the man struggled, grunting and shouting through the tape on his mouth. John shook his head.

"I'd save your energy if I was you."

After one final straining effort, the man finally stopped struggling and sat still.

They sat in silence. John felt his eyelids growing

213

heavier. He had no idea of the time, but he guessed it must be late. As he began to feel his eyes close, the metal shutter slid noisily open, and in walked Nick.

Nick slid the shutter closed and picked up a folding chair from the corner and carried it to the small desk. The two captives watched him as he did it without looking at either of them. He opened the desk and took out a bottle of whiskey, placing it on the top. Still acting as if he was the only person in the room, he walked to the far corner and knelt down at the safe. Turning his back to block any view they may have, he entered the codes and opened the door. The top half of the safe was empty. Not a single note of the money stash was there. For a second, Nick filled with dread. But then, he realised, it no longer mattered. The only person who could possibly have figured out about this place was Lisa. He didn't know how she had done it, but she was clever enough and knew him well enough to have figured it out somehow. He didn't need the money now. He was beyond that, but Lisa might need it. For Monica. So he was glad that she had found it. Before it was too late.

He took out the gun and closed the safe. Nick heard Scott let out some sort of groan as he carried the gun over to the desk. For the first time now, Nick looked over at the two men. Collins was looking at the gun, his dad looking impassively straight at him. Nick placed the gun on the desk and took the one he'd taken from the Georgian from his pocket, placing it on the desk alongside his own. He walked over to Collins and ripped the tape from his mouth, Collins letting out a little yelp as he did so. Nick walked back to the table and opened the whiskey, taking a swig from it. He walked over to his dad and held it to his mouth, but his dad didn't accept, so he went and sat down opposite the two of them.

"Here we are, then," he said finally. "Three monsters together."

"Who's this fucker?" John asked, nodding his head towards Scott.

"Who am I? Who the fuck are you?" he yelled back at

John. He turned to Nick. "And who the fuck are you?"

"You know who I am," Nick replied.

"Do I fuck!"

"Well, you know what I know, that's enough."

"Oh yeah, and what do you know?"

"I know what you did, Scott Collins. Or should I call you Beast?"

John watched the two of them talk back and forth like he was watching a tennis match.

"Are you in pain?" Nick asked Scott.

"Fuck you."

Nick picked up his gun and walked over to Scott, who kept his eyes on the gun but straightened himself defiantly up in his chair, making himself look as big as possible.

"Are. You. In. Pain?"

Still Scott said nothing. Nick placed the tip of the gun against Scott's knee and gently pushed it. Scott did his best to suppress a groan. Nick smiled.

"That leg's probably broken," he said. "The other one might be too. A few ribs, most likely, as well. Some internal bleeding, I bet. Yeah, you're in pain."

Scott spat in Nick's face. A thick, phlegmy wad, clotted with blood. Nick wiped it off with his sleeve and pistol-whipped him across the face. He knelt down to face him, putting his hand over his mouth.

"I'm glad you're in pain. Because I bet he was, wasn't he? He was scared too, wasn't he? Terrified, probably. In his last moments. Well, I know you're scared now. However much you try to hide it, I can fucking see it." Nick turned to his dad, who had been watching this exchange but with less idle curiosity now, with more interest. "I know all about fear, don't I, Dad?"

Collins's eyes flicked across to John at the word "dad", confusion again filling his eyes. Nick walked over to his dad, wiping the snot, spit and blood from his hand on John's pyjamas.

"Fear was bred into me right from the fucking start, wasn't it, Dad?"

"What the fuck do you think you're doing, lad? Where are we, and who the fuck is this fella?"

"This fella? Oh I think you'd have a lot in common with this fella. You both enjoy inflicting pain on people too weak to defend themselves."

"What are you on about, son? I don't understand this."

"This man," Nick pointed at Scott with the gun. "This man beat, raped and murdered an eighteen-year-old boy. He dumped his body in woods and left him to fucking rot." Nick moved over to Scott, looking at him as he continued to talk to his dad. "Fucking eighteen. Smart, beautiful lad with his whole life to live. And he snuffed it out."

"Fuck you, cunt. Fucking prove it," Scott shouted.

"I can't fucking prove it, can I? There's not enough evidence. But you and I both know. We're the only two living people who know. Until now, anyway."

Scott realised he was right. What he had done, what he had become since he let the Beast take over, he had been proud of it, but unable to share it with anyone. He had to carry the knowledge on his own. But this man knew what he was, knew what he had done, and, for the briefest moment, Scott felt some sort of odd kinship with him. But just as quickly as it appeared, that feeling was replaced by loathing. This man was weak, pathetic, scared. Scott was tied and taped up, and this guy had a gun. Two guns. But Scott could still sense the fear in him. Even if he knew what Scott had done, he wasn't capable of understanding what he really was, what he had become.

"Fuck him," Scott said, "fucking dirty little faggot got what he deserved. And as soon as I get out of these, so will you. You fucking pathetic little cunt. I'm gonna fucking destroy you. I'm gonna fucking rip you apart. I'm gonna make you suck my fucking dick before I crush your fucking skull with my bare hands. Fucking weakling."

"Ha! He's got you there, son. This guy must know you pretty well."

"What's that supposed to mean?"

"It means, son, what's the fucking plan here? You've

fucking kidnapped me, you've done fuck knows what to this one, you've got us tied up here, so what's next? Thing is, Nick, you and I both know you're not gonna go through with this. You're too fucking weak. Always have been. You're no fucking killer."

"You don't know me as well as you think, Dad."

"Oh, yes I do. You don't have it in you. You've always—"

Nick cut him off with a pistol-whip to the face. John spat out a mouthful of blood.

"What the fucking hell's wrong with you?" he spluttered. "I'm your father. I'm your fucking father."

"Don't I fucking know it? I know you're my fucking father, that's the fucking problem. It's all down to you. You made me this way, you made me as bad as him."

"Oh fucking grow up, Nick. Fucking pathetic, whining, little prick. Fine, you wanna kill me, then fucking kill me."

"He hasn't got the fucking guts," Scott shouted, "the little faggot."

"Shut the fuck up!" Nick shouted, shoving the gun in his face.

"Little nancy boy," John yelled.

"You shut up too, Dad."

"Fucking weakling."

"Pansy."

"Shut up, shut the fuck up, both of you."

Nick moved away and put his hands over his ears.

"Come on, fucking do it, fucking shoot us both, Nick."

"Do it, come on, faggot."

"Show me what you're fucking made of. Make me proud."

Nick screamed, lifted the gun and fired.

THIRTY-FIVE

John wouldn't tell them what had happened. The police had been out looking for him but it was one of the staff that found him. He was sitting on the bench outside the front entrance, shivering in the cold. When the police came back to question him, he insisted he had no memory of what had happened. He was badly beaten and had pissed himself. A doctor came to look at him and said he'd need to be taken to A&E but John refused, at least until he had been to sleep for a while. The staff cleaned him up, the doctor gave him some painkillers and tended to his wounds, though he was certain John would need some orthodontic surgery. The staff had been frantically trying to contact his son but he couldn't be reached either on his mobile or the work number they had. John told the staff not to bother him, that he was probably out of town with work, and he was sure he'd be round to see him soon.

Two days later, the manager received a letter from Nick Hanman informing him that, due to unforeseen circumstances, he would not be renewing the contract for his father's residence at Cedar Nursing Home at the end of the current financial year, and asking them to instruct a social worker to find alternative accommodation.

*

Paul Jenkins had received the phone call at three in the morning. He had only been in bed for an hour and a half. The desk sergeant at the station hadn't made much sense. Something about a confession to the McGann murder. They didn't get too many nuisance false confessions, but it certainly wasn't unheard of.

As he walked into the station, Sergeant Evans ran out from behind the desk.

"Where is he then, Evans?"

"He's at the hospital, sir."

"The hospital? Why is he at the hospital?"

"I explained on the phone, sir," Evans said.

"I was fast asleep when you rang and I'd had a few pints before bed, so what you said made fuck all sense to me. All I got was that someone had come in and confessed."

"Well, not exactly, sir."

"Not exactly? Did someone confess or didn't they?"

"Sort of."

"Sort of? Evans, I'm not in the fucking mood for this. Just tell me what happened."

Evans told him he had been sat at the desk, nothing had been happening all night, but that sometime after two in the morning, he had heard a car outside and the horn beeping repeatedly. When he went out to investigate, the car had gone, but on the steps was a man, beaten, tied up and with a bullet in each kneecap.

"Alright," Jenkins said, "this sounds like some sort of gangland shit. What does it have to do with my murder case?"

"He had a written confession, sir."

"What, a man with both kneecaps shot up and tied up happened to be carrying a written confession to a murder?"

"No, sir. It was stapled to his forehead."

"Fuck me."

THIRTY-SIX

Nick let himself silently into the house. It was nearly four in the morning. Still dark as night, but it wouldn't be for long, so he knew he didn't have much time. First he checked on Lisa to make sure he hadn't woken her. He stood over her as she snored gently away, and wondered how many times he had slipped stealthily into this house at this sort of time and slid into bed next to her. How many times she had fallen asleep without him there, and woken to see him only briefly before he left again. Sometimes he'd be gone before she even woke up. Now, he knew he would never be joining her in that bed again. He pushed the door closed and went through to Monica.

She was curled up on her side, the blanket half on, half off, her arm curled around her favourite cuddly toy. He sat down on the floor beside her bed and covered her with the duvet. He watched her sleep. She was four years old now, and he quickly guessed that he had probably been absent from her life for about two and a half of those, and when he had been here, half the time he had been drunk, high, hungover or at the very least distracted. Sitting and watching her, he realised he had never allowed himself to be fully emotionally there, fully in the moment, with his focus entirely on his daughter, for anything but the rarest of occasions. He had been a desperate, hopeless failure of a father. Not once had he appreciated what he had in front of him. Only now, here on the floor, in the early hours, with his daughter deep in sleep, did he truly realise just how much he loved her. He wept. He wept for Monica, for the times she had needed or wanted him and not had him there. He wept for Lisa, who had tried again and again to reach him, to drag him back from the precipice, who had tried to love him but been shut out again and again. He wept for his mother, driven to suicide by a brutal husband, and who didn't have enough to live for, because all she had was him, a pathetic weakling of a son who didn't protect her. He wept for Christian McGann, who had been ripped from this world so brutally, and who Nick had failed because he didn't have the guts to administer the kind of justice Christian deserved, instead dumping his killer with the police, with a confession that he knew would probably never stick. And he wept for himself, because there was nothing else to do.

He kissed Monica on the head, whispered to her that he loved her, hoping that it would somehow seep into her unconscious, and left her room.

Before he exited the house, he left an envelope on the hallway table. Inside was a letter he had written to Lisa attempting to explain himself, and another one for his solicitor instructing him to ensure that, as well as everything he owned being left to Lisa as per his will, his business be sold to the highest bidder and the proceeds to also go to Lisa and Monica. Inside a plastic bag which he taped to the second letter was a memory stick with all the company's account and client details on it.

As the very first signs of the rising sun began to break through the windows, he left the house for the final time.

*

Twenty minutes later, Nick parked in his space, grabbed his gym bag from the boot and took the employee lift up to the building lobby. Clive was dozing at his desk, but looked alert when the lift doors pinged open.

"Evening, Mr Hanman," he said.

"Evening, Clive. Or morning."

Clive looked at his watch.

"Oh, yeah, morning. Of course."

"Anyone else working late? Or early, should I say?"

"Just me and you."

Nick nodded and began to walk back to the lift.

"You alright, Mr Hanman?"

"What's that?" Nick said, taking a few steps back towards the front desk.

"You look tired."

"I am tired, Clive. I'm really tired. Have been for a long time, actually."

"You should get some rest."

"I will, Clive. I will. Very soon."

"Oh, I almost forgot, that detective came by again. The one who was here the other day."

"Oh yeah?"

"Yes. Said he'd catch up with you soon."

"Yeah, I expect he will."

He walked back to the lift and took it up to his office floor. Again, he was surprised Michael hadn't ordered the locks to be changed or for his company name to be removed from the door and signs. He let himself in and sat at his desk. He composed an email to Kathleen, thanking her for all her hard work over the years and apologising for not being a better boss and for leaving her in the lurch now. He attached a reference letter for any prospective future employer, then scheduled the email to send in two hours' time, on the off-chance it would wake her now and she'd call the police. He logged into one of his bank accounts and set up a transfer to Kathleen's bank account. It was equivalent to six months' wages, enough to tide her over.

He shut down his PC, picked up the bag and took the lift up to Michael's floor. He easily picked the lock into the main office, and again into Michael's private office. He switched the light on, went over to the drinks cabinet and poured himself a tumbler full of bourbon. He sat at Michael's desk and knocked it back before filling it back up. He looked around Michael's office, the enterprise and community awards, the photos with the famous and influential. He wondered whether anyone other than himself truly knew who Michael Epson was, what he really was. He cursed himself for never having compiled anything to use against him. He had never kept any pictures, never taped any conversations, never even thought to keep anything in reserve. He had no legitimate course of retribution against him now, only the course of action he had chosen. That's what made Michael's decision to send someone to kill him all the more stupid. There was nothing Nick could do to expose him. He drained his glass and unzipped the bag. He took out three of the plastic bottles filled with petrol, placing one on the desk, another in the middle of the floor, and emptied one over the sofa. The fourth one, he opened and poured it in a long trail towards the outer office. He took the lift down to his own office and did the same, before taking the lift back down to reception.

"You absolutely sure there's nobody else working at the minute, Clive?"

"A hundred percent."

"No cleaners in anywhere?"

"No, they won't be in for at least another hour."

"That's good. You should get going too, Clive."

"Get going?" Clive asked. "But I'm not finished yet. I don't hand over to Frank till six."

"I know, mate. But you should leave. You need to get off."

Clive let out a nervous laugh.

"Mr Hanman, I can't. I can't leave the building until I've handed over to the next guard on duty."

"Listen, Clive. I'm serious. This isn't a wind-up. You have to go."

"Mr Hanman, I'm serious too. I can't leave yet. I'm not leaving."

"OK. I'm sorry about this, Clive. But you've not left me much choice."

Nick reached into the back of his trousers and pulled out the gun.

"What are you doing?"

"Clive, I'm sorry. I didn't want to do this, but you need to leave the building right now, OK?"

"Why? What's going on?"

"You'll find out soon enough. Don't worry, nobody is going to get hurt. Not as long as you leave now."

"I don't suppose I have much choice, do I?"

"You don't."

Clive slowly walked out from behind his desk, picking his coat up as he did so, and edged towards the exit.

"And Clive? Can I ask a favour of you?"

"What?"

"Don't call the police yet. Just give me ten minutes?"

"Why?"

"Please, Clive. Just ten minutes. You can tell them I threatened to come back for you if you called them straight away."

Clive nodded his head and walked through the door, looking back through the glass as it closed behind him. He stood uncertainly for a moment before moving out of sight. Nick sprinted to the lift and went back up to Michael's office. He took out the lighter and lit the trail of petrol he had left at the outer reception area. He watched the flame pass quickly along the carpet, quicker than he had anticipated, towards Michael's office. Deciding it would be safer to leave the lift, he took the stairs, running down to his own office, where he repeated the act, waiting until he was sure the fire was beginning to spread before taking the stairs all the way down to the parking area. He jumped into his car and started the engine. He turned to the left to see Francis back in the passenger seat. They stared at each other for a moment before Nick put it into reverse.

He drove out of the car park and towards the rising sun.

Out of the night.

Out of the city.

If you enjoyed *Out of the City*, why not try our other Armley Press titles available from Amazon and through UK bookshops?

Ray Brown: *In All Beginnings*
ISBN 0-9554699-6-1
Mark Connors: *Stickleback*
ISBN 0-9934811-2-3
A.J. Kirby: *The Lost Boys of Prometheus City*
ISBN 0-9934811-5-4
John Lake: *Hot Knife*
ISBN 0-9554699-1-6
John Lake: *Blowback*
ISBN 0-9554699-4-7
John Lake: *Speedbomb*
ISBN 0-9554699-5-4
John Lake: *Amy and the Fox*
ISBN 0-9934811-0-9
M.W. Leeming: *Justice is Served*
ISBN 0-9934811-4-7
Mick McCann: *Coming Out as a Bowie Fan*
ISBN 0-9554699-0-2
Mick McCann: *Nailed*
ISBN 0-9554699-2-9
Mick McCann: *How Leeds Changed the World*
ISBN 0-9554699-3-0
Chris Nickson: *Leeds, the Biography*
ISBN 0-9554699-7-8
Nathan O'Hagan: *The World is (Not) a Cold Dead Place*
ISBN 0-9554699-9-2
Samantha Priestley: *Reliability of Rope*
ISBN 0-9554699-8-5
David Siddall: *Breaking Even*
ISBN 0-9934811-1-6
K.D. Thomas: *Fogbow and Glory*
ISBN 0-9934811-3-0

Visit us at www.armleypress.com and look for Armley Press on Facebook and Twitter